Worthy is Your Child

Richard Polzin

Worthy
IS THE
Child

32
Moral, Uplifting Stories
to Change You and Your Child's
Life Forever

RICHARD POLZIN

Illustrated by
Richard and Sharon Polzin

DEDICATED TO
ANNA LAURA, JUSTIN AND ZACHARY
You made our lives complete.
— *Richard & Sharon Polzin*

Worthy is the Child © 1995

by Richard Allen Polzin

Illustrated by Richard A. & Sharon M. Polzin

First Edition

ISBN 0-9645911-0-3

Published by Nite Lite Stories, Inc.

P. O. Box 12283

Jackson, MS 39236-2283

Designed by John Langston

CONTENTS

SALTINE THE QUACKER & MO

A seven year old can love things one day and hate them the next. That is how it was with Jenny. She loved school; she hated school. She loved her little brother; she couldn't stand her little brother. She had more friends than anybody; she didn't have one good friend in the whole world.

However, there was one thing Jenny never changed her mind about and that was Mo, the biggest, most lovable Great Dane in all the world. Wherever Jenny went, Mo was at her side, his tail wagging and begging for attention.

One day Jenny's world came to an end, or so she thought. Her father's job required them to move to a big city across the country. She would miss living in a small town, but most of all she would miss the rolling hills where she and Mo would roam for hours and hours.

Finally the big day came, and Jenny's family loaded up and headed west. For three days they drove past towns, mountains and even deserts until finally they came to their new home. It was a nice neighborhood. The people were friendly and Jenny quickly made new friends. Moving was not nearly as bad as Jenny had thought.

What about Mo? Well, he quickly made himself at home. As long as he was with Jenny, it really didn't matter to Mo where they called home.

One day while Jenny was at school some of the neighbors came over to visit with Jenny's mother. "Mo is too big, he scares my children," was one neighbor's complaint. Another asked her nicely to please keep him locked up and then added, "It is against the law to let animals run free." Jenny's mother apologized and said that Mo would no longer be allowed to run free.

That night after supper, Jenny's mother sat down with her and explained why Mo would have to stay in the backyard or on a leash whenever she went out with him. They lived in the city now, and country rules had to be left in the country. Neither Jenny nor Mo liked these new rules, but rules were rules, and they made the best of it.

After lunch one day, Jenny's best friend, Mary, who lived next door, invited her over to see her new pet duck she had gotten for Easter. Saltine was his name and quacking was his game. He was so cute and noisy, and the girls played with him the rest of the day. "It sure would be nice to have a duck," Jenny thought, but she knew that dogs and ducks didn't mix well together.

One afternoon there was no one to be found and Jenny and Mo just stayed in the backyard and played. Jenny then decided to let Mo run free in the woods behind their house even though she knew he wasn't supposed to. "But who could he scare out in the woods?" she thought. Jenny opened the back gate, and Mo took off. It sure was good to see him run free again, but before too long Mo returned.

Jenny noticed Mo had something in his mouth, something white. "What could it be?" she thought as she ran toward Mo. Her eyes got as big as saucers when she saw Mary's dead duck hanging limply in Mo's mouth. "Mo, what have you done!" Jenny shouted. "There's going to be more than one dead duck around here when Mom finds out what I've done," she thought.

After a quick game of "I've Got the Duck and You Can't Get Him", Jenny managed to get Saltine away from Mo, and went inside. She had a plan. Jenny carefully washed all the dirt and grime off Quacker and blow-dried his feathers. Then quietly she went over to Mary's house and put the duck back in his cage. "When they come home, they will just think the duck died," Jenny thought, "and Mo and I will be safe with our secret."

The minutes seemed like hours as Jenny waited by the hole in the fence for Mary to come home. When she heard Mary's back door slam Jenny stood up to peek through the hole. As Mary's eyes caught sight of the cage and what was in it, she started screaming. Her parents ran out to see what was happening and quickly went to Mary's aid. Jenny had never heard such an outcry. She had expected them to be upset, but not this upset. Jenny felt so bad inside, and knowing she had to go over to Mary's house only made her feel worse.

Jenny's heart raced as she opened the gate. "I know you are upset, Mary, we all loved Saltine, but he's still just a duck."

"Just a duck," Mary shouted, "that duck died yesterday and we buried him in the woods, and now he has come back!"

Jenny's plan of deception had not worked. She knew she had made a terrible mistake. "If she had just told the truth instead of a cover-up, none of this would have happened," she thought. At first Mary was very angry with Jenny as she told the truth, but before long she began to laugh.

To tell the truth can hurt just a little, but to tell a lie can hurt for a lifetime.

O'MALLEY'S FORGIVENESS

There was once a proud, young Irishman named O'Malley, who lived along the Columbia River in the Great Northwest. One day he happened to be in the wrong place at the wrong time and was accused of stealing a horse. O'Malley would never have committed such a crime, but he was unable to prove his innocence; therefore, he was sent to prison. While in jail he became a hard, embittered man and never wanted to be around people again. So when he was released from jail, O'Malley left for the mountains to live alone forever.

Every morning O'Malley would head to the forest to chop down trees. Being a lumberjack was all he wanted to do in life. As he cut down the trees, he would mark the end of each log with an "O" for O'Malley so the sawmill would know it was his tree. After marking the trees, O'Malley would roll them down the mountainside into the Columbia River, and off to the sawmill they would go.

Every fall before the winter snows set in, O'Malley would take a week off from cutting trees and head deep into the woods in search of food. Winter in the mountains was very hard, and it was important to stockpile meat. It was not uncommon for a blizzard to trap him inside his cabin for weeks at a time, and the stored food would be used for such occasions.

Well, the hunting was good, and before long O'Malley had all the meat he could carry back to his cabin. With plenty of food for the winter, he was feeling quite proud. As he caught sight of his cabin, he could just taste a big, fine venison steak and feel the warmth of a roaring fire. However, as he started a fire in his fireplace, he noticed the smoke was not going up the chimney, but quickly filling the cabin. O'Malley ran outside coughing. He looked up on his roof, and there to his surprise was a big, purple bird sitting on top of his chimney. He tried scaring the bird by shouting and screaming. He even threw some snowballs at it, but the bird just sat there. "Well, there is only one thing to do," he thought. With gun in hand, O'Malley was ready to remove that bird once and for all.

Slowly he raised his gun and took careful aim. Just before squeezing the trigger, he heard someone shout, "Stop, don't shoot that bird." He lowered his gun as he saw a Forest Ranger running toward him. "That's the only Purple Crested Chimney Stork left in this entire area, and they are very rare," the Forest Ranger shouted.

"I don't care what kind of bird it is. That bird is coming off my chimney," O'Malley demanded. "I'm hungry, cold and want to be left alone."

O'Malley raised his gun and slowly took aim again. "If you shoot that bird you will go to jail," the Ranger shouted. O'Malley knew all about jail and did not want that again, so he grudgingly lowered his gun. "I'll come back tomorrow with some help," the Ranger explained as he left.

O'Malley couldn't believe that he had to build a fire on his front lawn and set up camp there for the evening. This didn't please him at all, but he wasn't going to break the law, at least not yet.

The next morning O'Malley awoke to the sound of wagons, horses, and people. Never had there been so many people on this side of the mountain. Before the day was through, the townspeople had built a fine new chimney on the other side of O'Malley's cabin and filled his cabin with fine meats, corn meal, and every kind of pie imaginable. At the end of the day all the people, including O'Malley, celebrated and danced the night away while the Purple Crested Chimney Stork sat atop the chimney.

The townspeople were so excited to have a Purple Crested Chimney Stork to call as their own, and journeyed up the mountain to check on this rarest of birds every day. They would often bring friends and relatives as they continued to shower O'Malley with food and homemade gifts. O'Malley would never have admitted it, but he liked all the attention he was getting that winter. The Purple Crested Chimney Stork and the townspeople had become his friends.

As the winter months passed and spring unfolded, five baby chicks started peeking their heads over the nest. O'Malley was afraid some crusty old hermit might do them harm if they left the safety of his cabin. So that summer O'Malley and his friends built five more chimneys around his cabin, one for each new baby stork.

The friendship of the storks and the townspeople slowly melted all the bitterness of the past, and O'Malley's heart was full of love again. His life now had a new purpose and meaning all because he changed his attitude from hate to forgiveness.

BILLY BUCK & SAWTOOTH

*B*eing twins was a blessing and a burden for Billy Buck and Sawtooth. Everyone was always comparing them to each other even though they were each unique and different in their own way. Everyone liked Billy Buck because he was outgoing, friendly, and fun to be around, while Sawtooth was quiet and gentle with a strong desire to be the best lodge builder in their colony. Yes, Billy Buck and Sawtooth were beavers, the largest rodents in North America. They both were four feet long and weighed 70 pounds each. That's a lot of Beaver.

As time went by, Sawtooth kept reminding Billy Buck that he needed to learn how to build a lodge and fend for himself because one day he would have to go out on his own. Well, Billy Buck was having too much fun, and besides, he had plenty of time to learn such boring skills.

Billy Buck's time ran out quite suddenly one day when some conservationists came into their colony and grabbed Billy Buck and Sawtooth. They put them into separate cages, and for the first time in their lives, they were alone, frightened, and separated from each other. The men planned to relocate the beavers on a river where there were no beavers. They knew that beaver dams were helpful in preventing flooding. The dams would also create ponds that other animals could use for drinking and natural havens for birds and fish. The conservationists were hoping Billy Buck and Sawtooth could start a new colony elsewhere.

The next day Billy Buck and Sawtooth saw each other while they were being loaded into an airplane. The plane's engines started and their great adventure had begun. After being in the air "forever," the cargo door opened, and their cages were pushed out of the plane. The beavers clutched onto their cages, not knowing what would happen next. With a loud flutter and a quick jerk, the excitement of the fall was suddenly halted when their parachutes opened.

As they fell aimlessly down to the ground they saw the most amazing sight, it was the beauty of the earth in its patchwork glory. Sawtooth could hardly wait to get back and tell the other beavers what he had seen, and then he remembered, he might not get back at all. With a bit of a thump, their specially designed boxes broke open upon impact and released the beavers.

"Wow, what a ride! It sure feels good to be free again," Billy Buck said

to.....to....."Where's Sawtooth?" he gasped. He ran through the woods looking for Sawtooth but he was nowhere to be found, and his excitement quickly diminished as he realized he was all alone and lost. The wind currents had blown the brothers in different directions and they landed miles apart.

Sawtooth was worried about Billy Buck, too. "I have always taken care of him and now I don't know what to do." He looked and looked for Billy Buck but to no avail.

As Billy Buck stumbled about the forest, he couldn't help but notice a change in the air. The bears were starting to hide in caves. The squirrels were feverishly gathering nuts and taking them to their nest. And the sky was full of birds, all heading in the same direction, SOUTH. Billy Buck had never noticed these things before. He was always so busy playing and having fun. What the other animals of the forest did to prepare for winter was none of his concern, until now.

Winter was quickly approaching, and since beavers do not have any defense against land predators, Sawtooth quickly started building a lodge for himself. Of course, Billy Buck was not prepared for such a change in life and just wandered around in the forest hoping to find his brother.

The weeks passed and Sawtooth had built a fine lodge and had stored enough food to last the winter. He still looked for Billy Buck every day, but he was nowhere to be found. Winter came quite suddenly one evening, and by the next morning, three feet of snow covered the ground. Sawtooth was warm and snug in his lodge while Billy Buck lay freezing in the snow.

Billy Buck realized that he would quickly freeze to death if he did not do something soon. As he lay shaking in the snow he remembered his father telling him that when in danger he should slap his broad tail on the water, because this loud signal could be heard all over the forest. With the little energy Billy Buck had left, he headed to the nearest pond and began slapping the water as hard as he could.

Sawtooth was busy storing more food for the winter, just in case he found Billy Buck, when he heard that most special of all signals and quickly rushed toward the sound. Just as Billy Buck was about to give up hope, Sawtooth appeared and rushed to his aid. Their reunion was joyful, but there was no time to waste. The winter's cold and the cry of wolves was everywhere.

Sawtooth quickly took Billy Buck into his powerful arms and hurried back to the lodge. Now Billy Buck was warm and enjoyed his first good meal in days. He was thankful to be alive and had learned an important lesson. From that day forward he would never put off doing things until tomorrow that were important today. He knew there was a time to play and a time to work, and in order to be a happy beaver, he must do both.

HAIR TODAY, GONE TOMORROW

Being sick is something nobody looks forward to, especially when you are seven years old. Now, just imagine being so sick that the medicine you have to take also makes you sick, a medicine so powerful and strong that you have to hook yourself up to a machine just to receive it. Every day for two weeks Zek went to the hospital just like he was supposed to and took his medicine; yes, he did get a little sick from his treatments, but overall he was getting better.

With seven treatments to go, Zek woke up one morning and noticed his pillow had a strange feel to it. As his hand reached up to smooth the pillow it came back with a fist full of his hair. Zek ran to his mother. "Mother, Mother," he shouted, "you said I might lose a little hair, but you didn't tell me my pillow would be full of it."

"I'm sorry, Zek. I should have been more honest with you, but I thought you had enough to worry about at first," his mother explained.

"What's going to happen; what shall I do? What will my friends say?" Zek went on. "I can't go to school like this," as he pointed to the balding spots on his head.

"When you finish your treatments and your hair starts growing back, you will look as good as new. Why not wear your baseball cap today, or at least until we can think of a better idea?" she added.

That morning Zek went to school because he had to, not because he wanted to. With his baseball cap securely in place, he walked out the door hoping his secret would be safe. During school that day Zek kept his cap on but realized that he couldn't wear a baseball cap forever. His hair was falling out so fast that he would soon be bald, and then what would his friends say. He dreaded the teasing, ridicule, and, most of all, looking different.

The final bell rang and school was over. "Thank goodness the teacher did not ask me to take off my hat. My secret is safe, but...what about tomorrow?" Zek thought as he dashed out the door and whirled his bike home at supersonic speed.

As Zek walked up the steps to his house, his mother greeted him with peanut butter cookies and a cold glass of milk. "When you finish your snack, I have an idea," his mother explained. Those cookies were eaten in world record time, and before Zek knew it, he was headed to the barber shop to get a crew cut. To cut all his hair off before it all fell out seemed like a great idea.

As Zek entered the barber shop, Mr. Bob greeted him with a friendly, "Hello, Zek. I'll be with you in just a minute." As Mr. Bob swung the barber chair around, there to Zek's surprise was Patrick, his best friend, with a crew cut.

"Patrick!" Zek shouted. "You've got a crew cut!"

"Right on," Patrick said as he rubbed his fuzzy head. "Look's cool, too, and feels great! Why don't you try one of these do's on?"

Zek looked at his mother with a big grin and replied, "I was just thinking about getting one myself."

Sitting in the barber chair watching his hair hit the ground was hard for Zek to take, but Mr. Bob had a great gift for putting children at ease while cutting their hair. As Mr. Bob was brushing Zek's neck, he turned to Patrick and said, "Crew cuts sure have been popular with the boys lately. You both look great!"

With their new crew cuts finished, Zek and Patrick spent the rest of the afternoon playing in the park and soon forgot about their bald heads.

Zek woke up the next morning still not sure how his classmates would take his haircut, but there was no turning back. He kissed his mother good-bye and headed to school without his baseball cap. As Zek got closer to his classroom, he could hardly move his legs, and opening the door was the hardest thing he had ever done. Even taking the treatments wasn't this hard.

Zek slowly opened the door, and much to his surprise, he saw twelve of the most beautiful bald heads he had ever seen. All the boys in his class had crew cuts. Zek's heart swelled up, and some embarrassing tears quickly followed when someone said, "Come on in, Zek. Welcome to the Bald Eagle Club. Remember, bald eagles are not really bald but are mighty in their strength and courage." Zek walked in and proudly sat down with the best bald-headed looking friends one could have.

Zek did finish his treatments and soon after recovered from his illness, and yes, his hair did grow back. However, the crew cut remained with him forever, to remind him how the Bald Eagle Club transformed the worst day of his life into the most wonderful one ever.

LIFE IN THE FAST LANE

*P*rime Time was the biggest, baddest, fastest car ever to spin his wheels on a racetrack. His chrome was the shiniest, his paint the brightest, and his wheels the fastest; and he always won when he raced. The only thing Prime Time did not have was a friend. He didn't give it much thought, though, because he was too busy being the biggest, baddest, and fastest car in town.

One day while going down the street shining for all the world to see, Prime Time came to a stop light, and there at his side was the cutest little convertible he had ever seen. The minute he saw her his engine started running hot. Well, Pink Pearl liked Prime Time, too, so off they zoomed traveling up and down the highways together.

Prime Time told Pink Pearl, "I am so glad you are my friend. I have a hard time making friends at the racetrack." Prime Time was so kind and gentle that Pink Pearl could not understand why others didn't like him, until one day he invited her to the racetrack to see him win. He knew he was going to win because he always won. Now Pink Pearl could easily see why Prime Time was always alone with no friends.

As the race was about to begin, all the cars lined up in their assigned slots except Prime Time. He liked to be last, and make an entrance all his own, that way he would not be dusty and dirty when he won the race. Since he was the best, he felt he deserved his own grand entrance. This made the other cars very angry, but what really steamed their engines was the way Prime Time acted at the end of the race. Prime Time would make a big, braggy show by revving his engine and spinning his wheels and never speaking to the other cars. He was too busy showing his trophies to the cheering crowd to pay them any attention.

After the race Pink Pearl decided to talk to Prime Time. "You are as fast as lightening on the racetrack, but someday you will not be the biggest, baddest, fastest car around. Do you know what it feels like to lose a race?"

"I'm in my Prime, Pink Pearl. I've never thought about losing, much less what it feels like."

"You and I are friends because you are kind and considerate of my feelings but what about the other cars? They have feelings, too. They know what its like to lose and yet they still come back, despite the way you treat them. I wonder why?"

A BAD ATTITUDE DOES NOT CHANGE JUST BECAUSE THINGS GET BETTER; HOWEVER, THINGS WILL GET BETTER WHEN YOU CHANGE A BAD ATTITUDE.

Prime Time wanted to argue, but he knew she was right. He went home and gave some serious thought to how it might feel to loose. He had only been thinking of himself and he knew that caring for others is important.

The next day, much to the surprise of the other cars, Prime Time lined up with everyone else and said hello to each car as he passed. The other cars were so surprised. This time he did not make a big, braggy show when he won. He drove up to the stand and collected his trophy without all the engine fireworks. Prime Time started watching the other races and began taking an interest in how the other cars did as well; but most surprisingly of all, he even shared some of his secrets on how to race. Soon Prime Time had more friends than he could count.

Prime Time had learned a valuable lesson. Being a good winner is just as important as being a good loser.

Prime Time continued his winning ways, but he kept winning friends also because his style of winning was different. Different because he really did care about the other cars in the race, and they knew it. He quickly became the most popular car on the track.

One day Prime Time lined up as usual, but he noticed a newcomer in the race—Earl Slick. He looked and acted like he was going to be tough. The race started as usual with Prime Time taking the lead; however, halfway through the race Prime Time noticed Earl Slick coming up fast. This newcomer knew his business. As Earl Slick moved in to pass, Prime Time reached way down inside and gave it all he had. Only this time all he had wasn't good enough. His plugs just didn't have the same spark in them, and his tires didn't grab the road as well as they used to. He was getting old, and Earl Slick zoomed past him to the finish, leaving Prime Time in a cloud of smoke and dirt.

Prime Time felt his world had come apart and his bumper was dragging the ground. Now he knew how all the other cars had felt when they lost. He rolled back to the pit area feeling the weight of the world. "How could he face all of his new friends?" he thought. As he turned into the pit row, he noticed his friends waiting for him. They were all there because they loved and cared for Prime Time.

"True friends share your sorrows, as well as your joys," explained Pink Pearl.

Somehow, Prime Time didn't feel so bad anymore. He had lost the race, but had won something much more dear—friends forever.

THE PERFECT HUG

"Anna Laura, can you please bring me some orange juice?" her mother asked.

"Yes, Ma'am. I'll be there in a minute," Anna Laura replied.

Have you ever loved someone so much that you felt bad when they felt bad? Well, that's how Anna Laura felt about her mother. A lot of other girls in her class always seemed to talk bad about their mothers, but not Anna Laura. A warm hug, cookies and milk, and "How was your day?" greeted Anna Laura every afternoon when she got home from school. By going to work an hour earlier every day Anna Laura's mother was able to be home when she got off the school bus. What a difference it can make when you really try to show someone how much you love them.

Anna Laura quickly got her mother some orange juice, sat down beside her, and asked, "How are you feeling today, Mother?"

"Being sick is not quite so bad when someone you love is there to care for you," her mother answered.

"Mother," Anna Laura added, "Mariel said that she wished her mother could be home with her in the afternoons, like you."

"I know, honey. But not all mothers can get off from work an hour early. Their jobs just won't allow it. However, each of us can make what time we have with our families special. A soft word, a warm hug or just holding hands every now and then are gifts we are all capable of giving. Even if you have to pretend a little sometimes, when you treat someone special it won't be long before they start treating you special. You and I can be that example and just maybe some of the girls in your class will take a soft word or a warm hug home to their families. Now off to school you go, but first give me a big hug."

Anna Laura woke up the next morning with a great idea. "I'll break open my piggy bank, gather my pennies, nickels, and dimes, and head to town." She knew something new and pretty would make her mother feel better, so out the door she went. She just lived a couple of blocks from Main Street where the most wonderful shops were. Each shop put their best things in the windows hoping the passing shoppers would stop and shop with them.

As Anna Laura walked by a ladies' dress shop, the pretty red dress in the win-

dow caught her eye. "Why, that's just what my mother needs to feel better," Anna Laura thought. She opened the door, marched in, and proudly proclaimed, "I would like the red dress in the window for my mother."

"Well, that's fine, young lady. What size dress does your mother wear?" the saleslady asked.

Anna Laura thought for a moment, then lovingly answered, "She's just perfect. She's just perfect."

Another saleslady overheard the conversation and motioned for Anna Laura to come to her. She reached out and said, "Hug me like you would hug your mother and tell me if I hug the same. Together, maybe we can figure out your mother's dress size."

Anna Laura wasn't sure about hugging strangers, but she really wanted that red dress, so she hugged the saleslady just like she would hug her mother. "No, it just doesn't feel the same," Anna Laura answered. By this time, all the salesladies had gathered around and each one took their turn hugging Anna Laura. It was no use. None of them had that perfect hug, like her mother did.

The $6.21 Anna Laura had brought from her piggy bank was not nearly enough to buy that red dress. But $6.21 and 11 hugs was. The salesladies gathered their nickels, dimes and quarters and quickly took Anna Laura's red dress out of the window and wrapped it in their finest wrapping paper. With her gift in hand, Anna Laura softly said, "Thank you," and waved good-bye to the salesladies and headed out the door.

Anna Laura was so excited that she ran all the way home, right into her mother's arms. She proudly helped her open the finely wrapped package, and a perfect hug soon followed.

"Hurry, try it on!" Anna Laura beckoned.

"This is so beautiful and thoughtful but I need to wait until tomorrow to try it on when I feel better," answered her mother, as she reached across the bed and kissed the disappointment away.

The next day, while Anna Laura was in school, her mother went back to the dress shop and exchanged the red dress for a larger size—a much, much larger size. To a little girl, perfect hugs have nothing to do with shapes and sizes and Anna Laura's mother was not the perfect size by adult standards. But more importantly, she showed her love by sharing long walks in the park, ice cream sundaes, and bedtime stories with her daughter—and yes, lots of hugs. These are the things that make a perfect hug and a perfect mom.

BOOMER'S UNBEARABLE HEART

Wearing the crown "Most Beautiful Bear" and leading the cheers at Bear High football games were very important to Honey. You see, being the most popular honey bear in school was hard work, sometimes too hard.

One day a bunch of Honey's friends were sitting around eating some honeycomb when Boomer, the new bear in school, walked by. They all started laughing and making fun of him because he was different. His clothes were old and bearly fit, his fur was dull and matted, like he had slept in it all winter, and his shoes looked as though they had been caught in a bear trap.

Honey did not like making fun of Boomer, but she pretended to laugh along with the others. She liked being popular and wasn't going to risk her position to defend a stranger.

When Honey got home from school that afternoon she told her mother what had happened. Her mother put down her knitting and motioned for Honey to come sit by her. Mrs. Bear explained, "You and your friends should not judge someone by the way they look on the outside. We should bear our love to everyone. A cheerful smile and a word of encouragement would probably mean more to this little cub than anything else." In her heart Honey knew her mom was right.

Armed with her mother's words of wisdom, Honey headed to school the next day determined to show love and understanding to Boomer. During lunch Honey sat down and talked with Boomer, and much to her surprise, she found him to be quite nice and fun to be around. He was gentle, kind, and soft spoken. She admired his uplifting spirit. Even the unkind remarks of the other bears did not seem to ruin his day. She and Boomer soon became good friends.

However, the other bears continued to make fun of Boomer, and now they included Honey in their unkindness. Life became unbearable for her. She now had a choice to make, or so she thought, and she chose to go back to her old friends and not see Boomer anymore. Her friends quickly accepted her back once she had abandoned Boomer; but Honey's heart was heavy. There was heartache without Boomer, and there was heartache with Boomer. What should she do?

One evening Honey's mother told her about a widow bear in their town who was having a hard time feeding her family. A poacher had killed the Papa Bear for

his fur and the widow had recently injured her paw in a bear trap. With her crippled foot she could not find work to support her family. The Lady's Den had prepared supper for the widow bear and Mrs. Bear asked Honey if she would help deliver the food.

Honey was excited to help this family. After supper she hurried to the widow's house and found her to be very kind and gracious. The widow explained to Honey how unselfish her oldest cub was. She was so proud of the way he would get up early each morning and hunt for honey. Then after school, he would work well into the night attending to Papa Bear's chores. Honey could feel the deep abiding love the widow felt for her oldest cub.

Honey went to school the next day and shared the widow's story with the rest of her friends. They all admired the unselfish love the little bear had for his mother and the rest of his family.

That evening Honey could not wait to go back to the widow's house and pick up the platters and bowls she had left the day before. She wanted to show the widow how much she cared.

As Honey came upon the widow's house she noticed Boomer working in the field next to the house. While visiting with the widow, Honey mentioned that she had seen Boomer working outside. The widow's face lit up and with a tender, soft smile she said, "Boomer is my oldest son." Can you imagine how Honey felt? She cried all the way home.

As Honey ran into her mother's arms, she was reminded of her mom's words, "Bear your love to everyone." The next day at school, Honey apologized to Boomer for not being his friend, and soon after, the other bears accepted Boomer, too. The bears no longer judged Boomer based on his outside appearance. How he lived his life every day inspired them all. He was widely respected and became a great leader because perseverance through difficult situations made him stronger and better.

Honey was still popular, but for all the right reasons. She maintained her self-respect by doing what she knew was right despite what her peers were telling her. Being "Most Beautiful Bear" and leading cheers at the football games were still great honors which Honey enjoyed, but being an honorable bear and upholding the dignity of another bear was the best honor of all.

MAKING RAINBOWS

Zachary's dad was always up by 5:30 A.M. every morning and out of the house headed for the office before Zachary even thought about getting up. Mr. Mangum ran a very large company, and when he spoke, everyone listened. He was very busy all day long giving orders and making demands on everyone around him. His commitment to his job left very little time for his family.

Mr. Mangum usually got home from work around 8:00 P.M., just in time to tell Zachary good night; and on weekends Mr. Mangum played golf with his business associates and worked in his study most of the time. Zachary wanted his father to play ball with him but he knew his business came first.

Zachary's mother was his whole world. She fed him, cleaned him, and loved him every day. One day Mrs. Mangum held Zachary in her arms and announced that she was going to have to stay with her mother, Zachary's grandmother, for a week. "Your grandmother is sick and needs me, Zach," she explained. "Your father will take good care of you."

"But I need you, too," Zachary cried.

His heart was breaking as he watched her leave the next morning. She had arranged for him to stay with a neighbor, Mrs. Craft, after school every day until his father got home from work, but no one could replace his mom.

Zachary loved Mrs. Craft. She was a kind, gentle lady with a twinkle in her eye and smile on her face every time Zachary showed up on her doorstep. Since his grandparents had died several years ago, Zachary had adopted Mrs. Craft as his grandmother. He loved to help her pick turnip greens, tomatoes and radishes in her garden and she always had the biggest, fattest worms in her yard. Zachary enjoyed digging up the squirming rascals and storing them in a jar for future fishing trips.

He loved all these things about Mrs. Craft but today it wasn't the same. He missed his mother. It rained the whole afternoon, and the rain only made Zachary feel worse. Just before sunset the rain finally stopped, and Zachary went and sat on Mrs. Craft's porch. Realizing his sadness, Mrs. Craft brought Zachary a bowl of popcorn to feed the birds.

"Look at that pretty rainbow," Mrs. Craft declared. Well, Zachary looked at the rainbow, saw nothing pretty about it and gave no response.

"Zachary, did you know that in order to make a rainbow you have to have rain and sunshine? Right now you feel the rain inside, but there's a rainbow out there for you, too. In order to get your rainbow, you must let the sunshine come in." Zachary did not understand what Mrs. Craft was saying, but it felt good to know that someone cared.

Mr. Mangum finally came home a few minutes earlier than usual, but still late. He quickly set the pizza down, and they ate supper. Now it was time for homework, and Zachary's dad sat down to help him with some math problems. At first it was a little awkward. Being together was new to both of them. Slowly Zachary began to realize why his father was so successful in business. He was very smart.

Now came the hard part. With homework finished and teeth brushed, it was time for a bedtime story and a goodnight hug. The only problem was, Zachary's dad didn't know any bedtime stories—and big hugs, well, he had never had time for those either. Realizing his father's embarrassment, Zachary gave a big yawn, hugged his father, and said, "I'm really too tired for a bedtime story. Goodnight, Dad."

The next evening Zachary's dad came home at 5:00 P.M. Never had Mr. Mangum come home so early. At first Zachary thought there must be something wrong. However, to his surprise, things were looking better. In one arm his dad had a sack full of groceries, and in the other he had bedtime storybooks. They were going to cook steaks and share stories all night.

As the week passed, Mrs. Craft slowly noticed a change in Zachary. A change for the better. Zachary's dad came home early every day now, not because he had to, but because he wanted to. He found something much more important than personally taking care of every little detail at his office, he had found his son.

Saturday morning came quickly. Zachary's soccer team had the first game that morning. Zachary always hated going to soccer because all the other boys had their dads to cheer them on. However, today was different. Zachary's dad was going with him. What a difference it made in the way he played. He could see his dad's pride in him as he ran up and down the field. After the game Mr. Mangum put Zachary on his shoulders and said," Son, I will never miss another one of your soccer games."

The day finally arrived, Zachary's mother was coming home. After all the hugging and kissing, she noticed how close Zachary and his dad had become. "What have you two been doing while I've been gone?" she asked.

With a big smile Zachary thought about the afternoon on Mrs. Craft's porch and responded, "We've been making rainbows."

BERTHA, A WHALE OF A TALE

Bertha was a beautiful, blue whale, one of the largest animals on the earth. In fact, she would gain over 200 pounds a day until reaching over 100 ft. long and weighing approximately 200 tons as an adult. She was as big as a small ship. Her mother and father loved her with all their hearts and tried to live a life that would be a good example for Bertha. They knew their actions meant a whole lot more than their words.

Because she was so big and slow the other animnals in the sea made fun of Bertha. They always chose Bertha to be last on their team. Bertha's mother could see how upset her baby whale was getting. One day she snuggled up next to Bertha and explained, "Life would be so boring if everyone was the same size and shape. You were perfectly made with very special abilities no other fish has. Bertha, did you know that because you are a whale you have the keenest sense of hearing, above and beyond all the other animals and fish of the sea?"

Bertha sighed, "So I can hear them making fun of me at a greater distance. Big deal."

One day while Bertha was off feeling sorry for herself she heard a strange, unusual noise coming from the top of the water—tick tock, tick tock. She had to find out what that sound was. Up, up, up she went until she reached the top of the water, and to her surprise, there was a man just barely afloat. His boat had sunk during a violent storm, and he had been floating for two days hoping someone would find him.

Startled by Bertha's size, the man started to swim away, but finally realized that it was pointless. If Bertha wanted to hurt him, he could not stop her. So the man paused and thought, "Why is this whale following me everywhere?" He did not know that Bertha was fascinated by the sound of his watch.

The sun was setting, and the man was getting weaker by the moment. Bertha knew she had to help this man if he was going to survive. She swam under the man and picked him up on her back. Using her keen sense of hearing, Bertha heard the sound of a boat's propellers in the distance and swam toward the sound. By the time they reached the boat it was after midnight and the boat was dark and silent. Whoever was steering the boat would never see them because the boat had only its running lights on. Bertha knew she could not continue swimming alongside the boat until morning. The rapid pace of the ship would soon tire her.

The man said to Bertha, "What shall we do, my friend? If I do not get on this boat, it may be weeks before another ship comes this close, and I will surely die before then." Quickly Bertha nudged the man into her blow hole and with all the force she could muster, she blew the man onto the deck of the boat. Bertha was glad the man was safe, and she was very proud of herself.

Because she had a new spirit of thankfulness, the fish jokes no longer bothered her. Soon the other fish stopped joking entirely as they saw Bertha's special qualities. They admired her strength and courage in rescuing the man.

One day during a terrible storm Bertha lost her sense of direction and found herself beached on the seashore, and the people quickly gathered around. The village whaler was already sizing her up for the slaughter. Bertha was hopelessly trapped and knew that she would soon die.

All of a sudden the crowd moved back and Bertha could hear a loud engine. Everyone looked up, and there was the largest crane they had ever seen. The crane gently picked Bertha up and put her back into the water. As they untied the straps holding her, Bertha paused to thank her rescuers, and to her surprise she heard a familiar sound—tick tock, tick tock. The man driving the crane was the man with the watch whom she had saved from drowning. Bertha suddenly realized that because of her unselfish act of kindness, she had also received kindness.

As Bertha headed out to sea, her friend quickly jumped into a speed boat and caught up with her. He guided her through the channel and the dangerous rocks hidden just under the water. As they approached the open sea, the man lovingly reached out to Bertha and tied his watch onto her fin as a token of his gratitude.

Bertha, the Gold Watch Whale, as she was called, became a legend among sailors. She brought luck to those who spotted her, and always led their ships to huge schools of fish. Because she was the *Lucky Charm of the Sea,* the watch also brought Bertha luck, as no whaler would dare touch the Gold Watch Whale.

THE MORE POWER YOU HAVE OVER ANOTHER,
THE MORE YOU REALIZE HOW POWERLESS
YOU ARE WITHOUT A FRIEND.

AL-KAZAN'S SWEET ROLLS

A long, long time ago there was a land where the sun was so hot it glowed a bright red-orange as each day began. Its long rays made the sand appear to be endless, and to go on and on past the horizon. This was the land of the great Grand Sultan of Abadad. He ruled his kingdom wisely, but his word was the absolute law. No one dared question the Grand Sultan's power. To disobey him in the least could mean certain death.

You would think that the wealth and power of the Grand Sultan would make him the happiest person in his kingdom, but he was not. The Grand Sultan had no friends and no one with whom to share his deepest secrets. Everyone who came to see him either wanted something or came to beg for his mercy. Even his closest aides feared his power. He was, indeed, the saddest person in his kingdom.

Because he was so sad, the Grand Sultan had trouble sleeping, and many nights he would roam the Palace in search of a friend. However, no one in the Palace dared befriend the Grand Sultan for fear of making him angry.

One night while lying in bed, the Sultan decided to sneak out of the Palace dressed as a gardener. He just had to find a friend. He quickly changed from his royal clothes into those of a humble worker and left the Palace by way of a secret passage that only the Grand Sultan knew about.

It was two hours before sunrise, and the city had not yet begun to stir. As he walked the quiet streets, the silence only reminded him of his loneliness. Then off in the distance, the Grand Sultan could hear the soft sound of singing. It was a friendly sound, and he quickly headed toward it. To his surprise, the sound was coming from a bakery. The outer room was as dark as night with only a soft glow coming from way in the back. The Grand Sultan knocked on the door, and for the first time in his life, he was afraid to meet someone for fear he might not make a good impression. Without his royal robes, his stately crown, and his power over all, the Grand Sultan no longer felt grand at all.

"Kind Sir, what can I do for you?" Al-Kazan said as he opened the door to his bakery. "It's still early and I have no fresh rolls yet. But if you are hungry, come in, I will be glad to warm up some of yesterday's rolls for you."

The Grand Sultan shyly entered, and was immediately put at ease by the baker's friendly disposition. For two hours he watched as Al-Kazan happily made his rolls.

"Are these the same rolls that go to the Palace every day?" the Grand Sultan finally asked as he finished his fourth roll.

"Yes, indeed they are. Why do you ask?" Al-Kazan replied.

"These day-old rolls I have just eaten taste sweeter than those made fresh and delivered to the Palace every day," said the Grand Sultan. "I sneak a roll or two every now and then," he added, for fear of giving himself away.

As the sun came up, the Grand Sultan bid the baker good-by and promised to visit him every morning. The Sultan could not help admiring the baker. He was poor compared to the Sultan, yet rich in his enthusiasm for living. The baker had learned contentment in doing his best, and that was his reward in life. Al-Kazan enjoyed hearing about the Palace gossip and the worldly views of his new friend. They spoke freely to each other about their joys and their sorrows, just as good friends do.

Then one day the Sultan decided to tell the baker who he really was. He explained, "I am not a poor gardener, as I have led you to believe, but the Grand Sultan. From this day forward I want you to come to the Palace and be the Royal Baker. Your rolls shall forever be called, 'Sweet Rolls' and as a reward for your friendship, I will grant you anything in my kingdom."

Al-Kazan smiled as he stopped kneading his dough. Tiny streaks of white flour danced across his cheeks as the glow of the fireplace reminded both of them that it was too early in the day for such serious matters. He cleaned his hands and turned to his friend and answered, "I am very humbled that you would leave the Palace and come sit in my small, dark bakery each morning. Your offer of wealth has astonished me beyond words. Yet, as I ponder this offer, I wonder if all the wealth of your kingdom has made you happy. I think not, or you would not be in my bakery every day. What has made you and me happy has been our unconditional friendship. This is something which cannot be bought. You see, Your Majesty, you have already given me the most precious gift you could offer. You have given me yourself. My wish is that the gift of your friendship will remain here in my heart forever and ever."

The Grand Sultan was so pleased with his friend's response that they remained best friends for life. Throughout the years the Grand Sultan and the baker shared secrets and sweet rolls each morning in the dark, little bakery as the red, hot sun slowly started each new day.

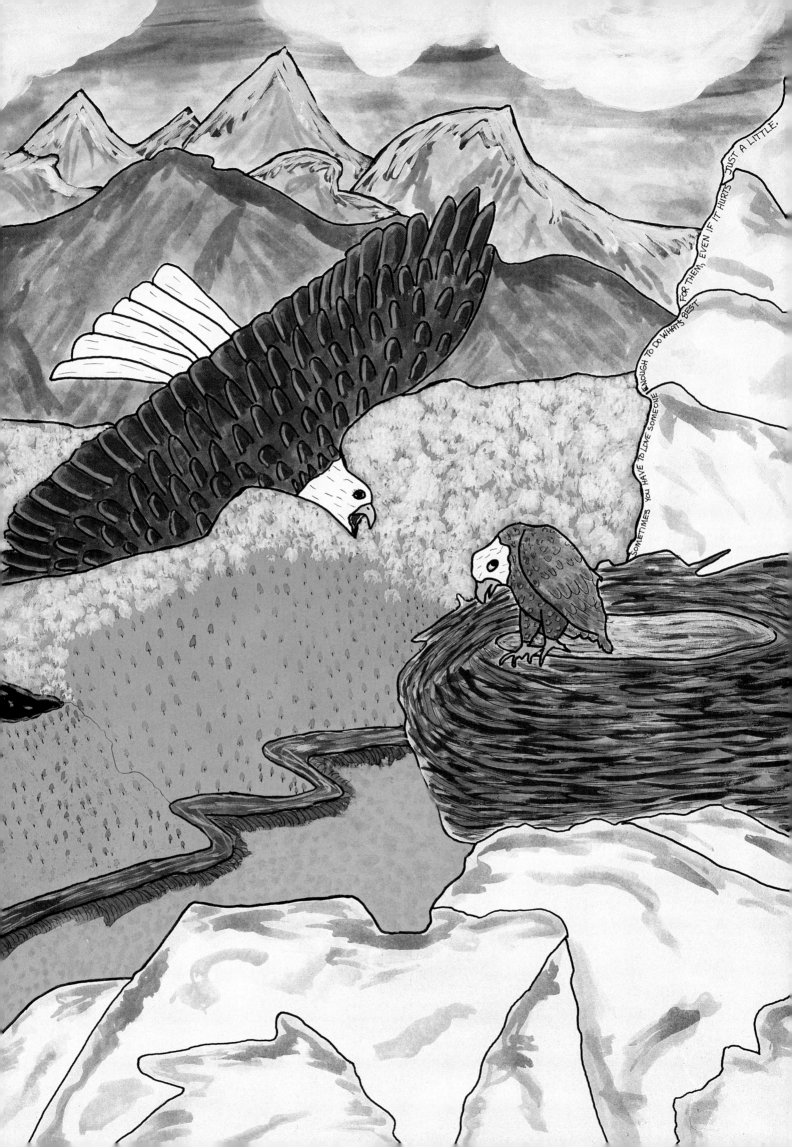

SOMETIMES YOU HAVE TO LOVE SOMEONE ENOUGH TO DO WHAT'S BEST FOR THEM, EVEN IF IT HURTS. JUST A LITTLE.

THE NEST OF THORNS

Mrs. Eagle was excited because soon she would have a little one to take care of. Building a nest on the side of a cliff, five thousand feet from the ground, would keep her busy for the next few weeks. Quickly she gathered the materials to build her home. Twisted limbs and thorny twigs were carefully arranged for the outside of the nest while inside she lovingly placed leaves, grass, feathers, and down from her soft underfeathers.

Then the big day arrived. Inside the nest was the prettiest egg Mrs. Eagle had ever seen. With patience only a mother could have, Mrs. Eagle sat on her egg until finally, Magellan came into the world. Hungry and scared, Magellan quickly reached for his mother. Kept warm by her presence and fed by his daddy, Magellan had little to fear and soon started enjoying his new world.

One day Magellan decided to take a peek at the world outside his nest. He carefully looked over the top of the nest but quickly dropped to safety. Magellan had never realized his home was so far from the ground. He looked up at his mother and asked, "Why is our nest on the side of this tall mountain?"

"We built our nest as high as we could for your protection. You are quite safe here," she gently explained.

"Safe," Magellan thought, "I'm terrified." Then Magellan had another question for his mother. "But Mom, why are we called bald eagles when we are not bald?"

His mother smiled, smoothed his feathers, and said, "That's right. We are not bald. However, our heads have white feathers, and our bodies have brown feathers. When we are soaring high in the sky, it looks as though our heads are bald." With a sigh of relief and his questions satisfied, Magellan settled down and soon forgot that he was five thousand feet in the air.

The warm summer days drifted by while Magellan grew bigger and bigger. Soon he filled the nest. Magellan had noticed that for the past two weeks his mother had been taking the leaves, feathers, and down out of the nest. She did not do this all at once, but each day she would take one or two items from the inner lining and discard them. At first Magellan paid little attention to his mother. But then the nest started feeling very uncomfortable; in fact, it was hurting him. Once the soft down was gone, the thorny twigs started sticking him. Magellan did not like it—no indeed!

YOU CANNOT MEASURE OR APPRECIATE ONE'S ABILITIES UNTIL YOU TRY THEM OUT.

Magellan asked, "Mom, why do you continue to remove the down from the nest? Don't you know that these sticks and thorns are hurting me?"

Magellan's mother replied, "I do it because I love you. Sometimes parents care enough to hurt just a little."

"How could she want to hurt me if she loves me?" Her answer did not bring comfort to Magellan at all.

Another week went by and Magellan continued to grow while his mother lovingly removed more down from the nest. Magellan was tired of being stuck by the thorns and decided he was going to fly away and leave his nest. Again he looked over the side of his nest only to drop down again. He was horrified and panic flooded his thoughts. "How can I just jump into the air?" What if my wings do not work? I DON'T KNOW HOW TO FLY!"

Magellan asked his mother a second time, "Why are you making the nest so miserable for me? Don't you love me?"

Again her reply was, "I do this because I love you."

Well, if this was love, Magellan wasn't going to have anything to do with it, and he brooded about it all night. The more he thought, the madder he got. By morning his mind was made up. He was going to jump, regardless of what happened.

Terrified but determined, he climbed to the edge of the nest, closed his eyes and jumped. As he began to fall, Magellan stretched his wings to their fullest and, all of a sudden, he was flying. He opened his eyes and felt a freedom he had never know before. This was wonderful. It was absolutely the greatest thing that had ever happened to him.

While he was still testing his wings, he caught a glimpse of his mother. She was smiling and waving to him. "I knew you could do it, Son," she cried.

Magellan's mother knew that words alone would not convince her son to jump into the air five thousand feet above the ground. Only Magellan could make that decision based on his desire to leave the nest and his courage to know that all things are possible. So, lovingly, she removed the comfortable lining from the nest. She loved Magellan enough to hurt him just a little.

A TOUGH NUT TO CRACK

*I*n the early days, being a farmer was very hard work. A mule and a hand plow were all a farmer had to help him till the soil. Caleb and his family did not have a lot of money, but were very rich in their love for each other and for their farm. They grew the best corn in Benson County, and Caleb's mother always won a blue ribbon at the State Fair for her corn pudding.

Just before noon one day the sky turned black, and the noise was deafening. Grasshoppers filled the air; millions and millions of them settled into the corn field. Within minutes they had totally destroyed the entire crop. Having the best corn in the county was very much to the liking of the grasshoppers.

With their corn gone, Caleb's family would surely lose their farm. The next day while walking through the woods Caleb came upon a family of squirrels. He resented their playfulness. "How can you be so happy?" he shouted.

Startled by Caleb's instant dislike for them, the squirrels scampered up the trees. That is—all but one little squirrel who stood before him as if to say, "Why are you so upset?"

Caleb realized he was taking his anger out on the squirrels. "I'm sorry, my friend," he said to the brave little squirrel. "The grasshoppers completely destroyed our corn and I am worried about my mother and father and the future of the farm." The squirrel seemed to understand what he said. He handed Caleb a pecan and quickly joined the others in the trees.

Caleb left, and as he walked home he thought about the squirrel family and how happy they were. "I wonder if my family will find that happiness again and if so, how?" As he approached the back door, he heard his mother and dad singing an old song that was playing on the radio. Caleb was puzzled as he walked in. "How could they be so happy with all their problems?"

His mother sensed his bewilderment and sat down beside him. "I don't know how, Son, but somehow we will make it through this hard time. I have found that happiness does not come from the absence of problems but in our ability to cope with them. Singing helps your dad and me cope."

Caleb told his mother about the squirrel family in the woods and how happy they seemed to be. She nodded her head and said, "You see, Son, the squirrels take life one day at a time. They work hard each day and store up food to carry them

THE VALUE WE PLACE ON THINGS IS OFTEN DETERMINED BY THE VALUE WE PLACE ON OURSELVES.

over during the hard times of winter. Your father and I also have stored up a little savings to hold us over for a few months until we can come up with another plan to save the farm."

Bright and early the next morning Caleb was awakened by the sound of something hitting his window. He got up, looked outside, and to his surprise his front yard was full of pecans. The squirrel family had been up all night gathering pecans so they could share them with Caleb and his family. Having gotten Caleb's attention, the squirrels quickly scurried back into the woods.

Word soon spread that Caleb's family had bushels and bushels of pecans to sell. In this part of the country wild pecan trees were very scarce and considered a real luxury. Within two weeks all the pecans were sold, and the farm was saved.

As winter approached, the pecan trees were yielding their final nuts. The selling of pecans had been so successful that Caleb continued to gather the nuts as they fell to the ground. At first, the squirrels were glad to see him, but after awhile they began to realize that Caleb was taking far more than his share. If Caleb did not stop, the squirrels would soon find themselves short of food for the winter.

Early one morning Caleb was about to leave the house with his pecan sack, when his father stopped him and said, "Son, the squirrels have been very generous with us, but now we must be considerate of them. We should leave the rest of the pecans for their families."

Caleb's father was a wise man. He had been thinking about the farm and about the pecan trees. "You know, Son, I think your squirrel friends have given me a great idea for our farm and our future. I have been reading about pecan trees. Did you know that it takes five years for a pecan tree to start bearing pecans? I think we should plant a pecan orchard on the farm. Also, because pecans are a tough nut to crack, we would never have to worry about grasshoppers again. What do you think, Son?"

"I think that is a great idea, Dad," Caleb shouted. "When do we start? Can I go tell my squirrel friends?"

"Yes, go tell them and we will get started right away," his dad replied.

Caleb ran to the woods to tell his friends. The squirrels were so excited that they helped Caleb start planting trees that very day. As he planted the trees Caleb realized, "Failure is not all bad, just don't let it defeat you. After all, without the loss of the corn field, we would never have started a pecan orchard."

LILLY'S SWAN SONG

*A*labaster was the whitest, fluffiest gander ever to float on a pond. He was busy all day making sure anyone who landed on or came near the pond knew just how important he was. Alabaster was king of the pond.

Nevertheless, quite unexpectedly one day, Lilly landed in the shallow water of the lagoon. She was a goose any gander would have been proud of. Quickly Alabaster swam over to Lilly, stuck his chest out, fluffed his feathers, and started flopping his wings as only Alabaster could do.

"Surely this will impress her," he thought. But just the opposite happened. Lilly was not impressed with Alabaster's importance at all. In fact, it caused her to shy away from him. Lilly was quiet and gentle and Alabaster's boastful ways did not impress her.

As the long, lazy summer days passed, Alabaster soon came to delight in Lilly's gentleness and she enjoyed Alabaster just being himself. It was so nice to have a friend that he could relax and be comfortable with, after all, putting up a front and always pretending in a way that's not natural takes a lot of hard work. The days just weren't long enough as they played together. Before long their bond was set, and the pond was no longer the most important thing in Alabaster's life.

As Autumn approached Alabaster found himself spending less and less time with Lilly. He had started some new projects around the pond and just didn't think about including her. This seemed a bit strange to Lilly because she hadn't changed, she was still gentle, quiet, and a bit shy at times. In fact, these were the things that had attracted Alabaster to her in the first place.

Then quite unexpectedly one day, a young swan flew onto the pond. Alabaster was excited to have a new friend to play with and quickly rushed over to show off. Once Alabaster was sure the swan knew he was king of the pond, he settled down and they began to play, only Alabaster decided the games and how they were to be played. But what about Lilly? Well, as you might guess, she was quickly forgotten altogether. Lilly watched them play day after day, and they never once asked her to join in.

A week passed, and Alabaster hadn't even noticed that Lilly had left and found a new pond to live on. Lilly still cared a great deal for Alabaster, but she no longer felt like she belonged, so she left.

Well, two weeks of playing according to Alabaster's rules were enough for the new swan, and he left as quickly as he had come. At first Alabaster didn't realize what had happened, but before the day was over, he felt more alone than he had ever felt in his entire life.

Day after day Alabaster searched for Lilly, but she was nowhere to be found. Finally, he realized that she was gone, never to return.

One day while he was feeling sorry for himself, Alabaster shared his sadness with the Wise Old Owl in the oak tree. "One day she just up and left me," he explained. The Wise Old Owl listened patiently as Alabaster blamed Lilly for everything that had happened. "What am I to do?" Alabaster finally asked.

"I remember the day Lilly landed on the pond. How excited you were," the Wise Old Owl explained. "You made time for her, you shared with her, but most importantly, you made her feel like she belonged. You were both as happy as you could be. But then you started neglecting your friendship. You only thought of your happiness and had nothing left for her. Every day I watched Lilly as she stayed in the shallow water hoping that you would include her in your fun. But you never did. Lilly is gone because her friendship was no longer valued."

The Wise Old Owl paused for a moment and then went on to explain, "To change the way you act and feel toward others doesn't happen overnight, but you can do it. If you want a best friend, you have to be a best friend." The Wise Old Owl's words were powerful and for several days Alabaster stayed off to himself so he could sort it all out.

Alabaster swallowed his pride and realized that the Wise Old Owl was right. Friendships are slow to grow, but quick to lose, and seldom last unless friends are valued for their feelings, thoughts, and desires.

As the seasons changed so did Alabaster, and word of his caring nature quickly spread through the forest. Lilly heard the good news and returned to see if Alabaster had really changed. It was true, Alabaster had changed. He was a wonderful friend and, yes, they did live happily ever after.

FREE AT LAST

"Time to get up, Jamie. School day," called his mom. Jamie could feel the energy in her voice, but his eyes would not open. A few minutes later and with a little more force she shouted, "Jamie, time to get up. If you don't get out of bed right now, I'm going to send your father up to get you."

"That sounds serious," Jamie thought. The last thing he wanted to hear was his dad's footsteps stomping up the stairs toward him, so sluggishly he fell out of bed and stumbled down the stairs.

A quick but friendly, "Good Morning," from his mother was followed by, "Come sit down for breakfast and be sure to finish all your cereal, including your milk. Here's your orange juice and vitamins, and when you get through, go straight upstairs, brush your teeth and get dressed for school."

Just once Jamie wished he could get up when he wanted to, eat what he wanted to eat, and school—forget it! Realizing this dream was impossible, especially this morning, he SLOWLY finished his breakfast and went back upstairs to finish dressing.

As Jamie reached for the front door, his dad's voice froze him in his tracks. "I told you not to wear that T-shirt with the holes to school. Now, go back upstairs and change shirts and put some socks on."

While Jamie was changing clothes, he thought, "That's it. I'm tired of being bossed around." So instead of going to school that day, Jamie headed for town. "Free at last. What a relief," he thought. "Nobody's ever going to tell me what to do again."

On his way to town Jamie crossed over a stream and realized how thirsty he was. As Jamie went down to get a drink of water, he heard a voice call to him from under the bridge. "Why, it's Benjamin—Benjamin from school," Jamie quickly realized. "Why are you hiding under this bridge?" he asked.

"I'm waiting for the *Born to be Free* Gang," Benjamin said. "They always come by here on their way to town. When I get up late and don't feel like going to school, I meet them here and have fun all day. Here they come, Jamie. This gang will show you the meaning of the word FUN."

Before Jamie realized what had happened, he and Benjamin were headed to town. "This is great! Now I'm going to be able to do just what I want," thought Jamie.

"The first stop is a grocery store," Blackjack, the leader of the gang, shouted.

As they were walking, Benjamin snickered as he whispered in Jamie's ear, "These guys can't even read so don't look or act too smart." Well, Jamie had never thought of himself as smart but he could clearly see a difference.

When they finally did stop at a store, everyone in the gang reached for the junk food. How they laughed at Jamie when he chose an apple.

Jamie's parents had always discouraged him from eating high calorie junk food. "It will rot your teeth," they would tell him. One look at the gang members rotten teeth was enough to convince Jamie that his parents were right. They couldn't eat an apple now, even if they wanted to.

"Why do they all seem to be so unhappy?" Jamie asked Benjamin.

"Unhappy? Why, they're not unhappy. Their parents let them do anything they want," Benjamin responded. Well, they were unhappy; Jamie could see it on their faces, by the way they dressed and in the way they talked about their parents. If this was freedom, Jamie didn't want to be a part of it.

Before long, Jamie began to realize that his parents must really love him. How easy it would be for them to do nothing and let him have his way. He knew he had made a big mistake. When the time was right, Jamie left the gang and headed home as fast as he could. It was getting late, and he knew his mother would have spent most of the afternoon preparing a wonderful supper.

Jamie entered the house as quietly as possible, but his mother could sense his presence. "Is that you, Jamie?" she asked. "Go upstairs, please, and wash your hands. Supper will be ready in a minute."

Earlier that day Jamie would have resented having to go and wash his hands. But now he knew some boys who would give anything to have someone love them—love them enough to care if their hands were clean. Jamie ran upstairs to wash his hands, and the steps seemed easier now. What a warm, wonderful feeling it is to know someone cares.

Jamie was free at last. Free because he now understood how much his parents loved him. The rules and responsibilities his parent enforced were not meant to restrict him but free him to grow into a healthy, responsible young man.

CHANGING HOUSES IN MIDSTREAM

*P*ot Belly Bob and Pretty Proud Pruddy were about the happiest possums in the woods. They lived in a big oak tree right next to the Lazy River with plenty of water, food, and friends. What more could they ask for?

One beautiful spring day Prudence was born. She was as pretty a possum as anyone could imagine. She brought great joy to the possums, and as the months went by and the seasons changed, Prudence was growing up to be a fine little possum.

While walking through the woods one day Prudence met a little black and white rabbit named Rupert. Rupert was crying and did not want anything to do with Prudence. So Prudence just sat on the log next to him, hoping somehow to make him feel better. After a few more sobs Rupert did feel better and stopped crying.

"My family had to move from the field where we have lived all our lives," Rupert explained. "One day the ground started to shake and the field was scraped clean by a great big bulldozer. I heard one of the men say that some human houses were going to be built on the field. I not only lost my home but all of my friends and my favorite hiding places. Now we live in the woods, and I am so unhappy here."

"I don't understand?" Prudence thought. "I have lived in the woods all my life and I think it is a great place to live."

Prudence decided she was going to change his mind about the woods and spent the rest of the day with Rupert. She showed him her favorite hiding places and introduced Rupert to all of her woodland friends. "Change is what makes the world exciting and new," explained Prudence. "It is okay to be sad about leaving your old home but give the woods a chance, they are really quite beautiful."

The sun was setting and Prudence had to get home before dark. As she started to leave, Rupert gave her a great big hug and said, "Thanks for such a wonderful day. I feel so much better."

While walking home Prudence had a warm, contented feeling because she knew Rupert was going to be okay. They had helped each other feel good about themselves and it was a wonderful feeling.

Early the next morning the Possums were awakened by the loudest, scariest sounds they had ever heard. The whining of chain saws and the rumbling of bulldozers filled the air. Then a man shouted from below their tree, "Cut this tree down. The road to the new houses is going through here." It didn't take five minutes for the man with the chain saw to saw through their home and destroy their lives.

The big oak tree gave a loud crack, and the man shouted, "Timber." As they hung on for dear life, the possums' home came crashing down. To everyone's surprise the big oak crashed into the Lazy River. However, the Lazy River was not so lazy. Its banks were filled to the rim by the heavy rainfall the night before. As the big oak tree hit the water, it was quickly swallowed up by the river's raging waters.

Pot Belly Bob and his family clung to the highest branches of the oak tree and did their best to ride out the fury of the river. Prudence was scared and crying.

"Hang on, Prudence. Whatever happens, don't turn loose of that limb," yelled her father.

The big, old tree tossed and turned in the waters. It was getting harder and harder to hold on. Then suddenly the tree gave a big jerk and Prudence's hands slipped, into the air she went and with a pounding blow, she landed on her backside. She quickly forgot about her sore bottom when she opened her eyes and realized that she had been thrown onto the shore and the tree was resting beside her on a large sand bar. The rest of Prudence's family quickly jumped ship also and found themselves in a strange new place. They were scared and exhausted from their ride and snuggled together inside a big hollow log for a long afternoon nap.

Pot Belly Bob held Pretty Proud Pruddy's hands, and with a big possum smile said. "We are going to be okay. We are still all together."

Pot Belly Bob found them a grand, stately new oak tree, not quite so close to the water, and in a matter of weeks things settled down and the family was pretty much back to normal, except for Prudence. She missed her friends and nothing seemed to make her happy.

While walking in the woods one day, Prudence came upon a tree with the words *"Rupert was here"* written on it. All of a sudden a warm, contented feeling came over her. She remembered the day Rupert and she had spent in the woods talking about his old home. Now it seemed as though Rupert was reminding her not to live in the past anymore. Prudence softly reached out and touched the tree as she said, "Thanks, Rupert."

Prudence grew to love her new home and friends. Change allowed her to welcome new, exciting adventures, as well as, store away those special memories of the past.

THE TUNNEL OF LOVE

*D*id you know that the state of Wisconsin is known as the Badger State? There are a lot of badgers in this part of the country, and Hannah and her family lived right in the middle of the Badger State. They worked long and hard on their dairy farm, and started each day bright and early at 4 A.M. This was her home, and she did whatever was necessary to help her family run the farm.

One day Hannah went into the barn and saw her dad building what appeared to be a trap. "What are you building?" she asked her father.

"Hannah, have you noticed all the holes in the pasture?" he replied. "We have a badger living near by. He is digging tunnels all over the fields, and when the cows step over the tunnels, they collapse, causing the cows to fall and break their legs. We have to get rid of the badger before we lose anymore cows."

Hannah's eyes showed her dismay. She knew the badger was a threat to the cows and to her family, but did this mean the badger must be killed, or could there be another way? Hannah did not want to see any creature hurt, even the badger. But Hannah knew her father loved them and only wanted to do what was best for the family.

The next day while Hannah was herding the cows toward the barn to be milked, she found one of the badger holes. The hole looked just like her father had described it. She peeked inside the hole and to her surprise she found a very frightened little badger caught inside the trap her father had built. Badgers had always been described to Hannah as mean and savage; however, all she could see was a helpless little animal with its leg caught in a trap. Hannah knew she had a decision to make.

"Please help me," the badger said gently. "I'm caught in this trap and it hurts."

Hannah tenderly explained, "I'm sorry you are hurt but your tunnels are collapsing in the pasture and causing great harm to our dairy cows. My dad put this trap here for you so that our cows would be safe."

The badger had no idea that her tunnels were causing so much trouble. She replied, "Why don't I just pack my bags and move down into the valley away from your land and your cows?"

"That's a great idea," Hannah shouted. She quickly released the trap and freed

the little badger. They parted friends and promised never to intentionally hurt anyone or anything as long as they lived.

Hanna paused and watched as the badger disappeared into the trees. She was glad that they were able to work out their problem peacefully and now she was ready to go exploring.

As she looked down into the valley she spotted an old abandoned well and quickly headed toward it. She had a splendid idea, if she leaned over far enough she could yell into the well and hear her echo. Very carefully, Hannah leaned over the side of the well. Just as she was about to shout, the sides gave way, and into the well Hannah slid. She fell aimlessly to the bottom of the well as a mountain of dirt and rocks fell with her. The dirt buried her all the way up to her shoulders. Confused and scared, Hannah began to cry and shout for help, but no one came. No one could hear her.

Several hours passed, Hannah had not come home for supper and her parents began to worry. It was not like Hannah to be so late. Her father realized that Hannah must be in trouble. His first thought was that she must have fallen into one of the badger holes out in the pasture. He ran to the fields, but Hannah was nowhere to be seen. His heart began to race as he heard a faint call for help coming from the old well. He ran to the abandoned well, and quickly realized that Hannah was in danger. The closer he got to the edge of the well, the more dirt tumbled down on Hannah. He knew that he would not be able to rescue her from the top of the well, but what was he to do?

The little badger was nearby and saw what had happened. Without hesitation, she started digging a new tunnel, and headed straight for the bottom of the well. Before long she had reached Hannah and quickly started digging the dirt away from her. Once Hannah was freed, she was able to follow the badger through the new tunnel to safety, and not a minute too soon, for the whole well caved in just as they entered the new tunnel.

It was a time of great distress for Hannah's parents as they saw the dirt settle, but before they could blink an eye, Hannah walked up from behind the well and gave them a big hug.

"Where did you come from?" they shouted.

"The Tunnel of Love," was her only reply.

GATESBY LAYS DOWN NEW TRACKS

Gatesby lived way, way up North; in fact, he lived so far North that it was winter all the time. Snow and cold were all he knew. That's okay, because polar bears like the cold, and Gatesby just happened to be a polar bear.

When you live this far North, the sun does strange things. Half the year is spent in total darkness, only to be followed by half a year of total sunlight. Many call it the Land of the Midnight Sun.

Gatesby loved the sunny time of the year because that is when his birthday came and for his birthday this year he got the most wonderful train set. The engine puffed real smoke and the whistle gave a fine toot. He could not wait to show it off to all his friends, especially Tucker.

The next day he invited Tucker over to play with his new train set. Gatesby really liked Tucker, and playing with him was always a lot of fun, because he always made Gatesby feel good inside. Gatesby anxiously waited and watched for Tucker from his room. Finally, Tucker pushed his way through the snow and was warmly greeted by Gatesby at the front door.

"Come on in, Tucker. I have a new train set in my room, and I want you to help me put it together," exclaimed Gatesby. They hurried upstairs and quickly tore open the box containing the new train set.

Tucker picked up the caboose, jumped on Gatesby's bed, and said, "This is the best train set I have ever seen. Everything looks so real. May I hook up the caboose?"

Gatesby shouted, "I need to hook up the caboose, besides it is my train, but you can watch. And that's my bed, nobody sits on my bed except me. You will have to sit on the floor."

"What a grouch," Tucker thought. "I wonder what is so special about his bed that only he can sit on it." So Tucker hopped down on the floor and tried to imagine what riding a real train would be like.

Tucker had a great idea and said, "Gatesby, why don't we run the tracks under the chairs and we can pretend they are large mountain tunnels."

Gatesby jerked the tracks away from him and explained, "Tucker, that's not what I want to do right now, maybe later."

Tucker sat on the cold floor and patiently watched as Gatesby put the tracks together and began to play with the train set. Tucker tried to enjoy and be a part of Gatesby's excitement; however, Gatesby would not share or take turns with Tucker at all. Tucker just sat there and watched the train go around and around.

Gatesby did not even notice when Tucker got up, left the room, and went downstairs. Feeling left out and rejected, Tucker went to Mrs. Polar Bear's sewing room. "Can I sit by the fire until my mother comes to pick me up?" he asked.

"Of course you can," replied Gatesby's mother.

Tucker reached into his pocket and pulled out an old toy soldier his father had given him a long time ago. Mrs. Polar Bear noticed that his toy soldier's uniform needed some mending. In no time, Tucker was mending and repairing his soldier with Mrs. Polar Bear's guidance. Oh, how proud he was of his soldier now.

Meanwhile, Gatesby was sitting on his bed all alone watching his train go around and around. He realized that he was not having any fun. "Where is Tucker, and why isn't he playing with me?" Gatesby thought. He jumped off the bed and ran downstairs, crying to his mother.

Mrs. Bear cuddled Gatesby in her arms and affectionately said, "I am so happy that you realized your friend Tucker is more important than your train set. Sharing makes us smile on the inside, as well as on the outside. Having a special friend to share a new toy with is truly a great joy." Well, that is not what Gatesby was feeling at all, but he soon realized that sharing would be better than playing by himself.

Eager to see the situation improve, Tucker asked Gatesby, "May I go upstairs and make the smoke stack puff and the whistle blow?"

Gatesby put his arm around him and replied, "I'm sorry for the way I acted. I will try to be a better friend." They both ran upstairs, hopped on Gatesby's bed, and took turns driving the train. The hours quickly passed, and before they knew it Tucker's mother was downstairs waiting to take him home. The two friends hugged each other and promised to always be best buddies.

The little bear had learned that the desire to share his things with someone else did not come easily. But because he worked hard and practiced sharing every day, before too long it came naturally. His reward was a best buddy forever and ever.

THE FOUR LETTER WORD

One day while playing on the playground, Taylor met some older boys. They were a little rough in the way they played ball and in the words they used but in a strange way Taylor was attracted to them. At first the boys would have nothing to do with Taylor and his innocent ways, but after several despairing looks Taylor convinced them to include him in their misadventures. Then it happened. The FOUR LETTER WORD.

One of the older boys had tripped over a rock and out of his mouth came the FOUR LETTER WORD. Taylor had never heard such a word before. It sounded strange and, he felt a little uncomfortable when he heard it. Taylor wanted to ask what the FOUR LETTER WORD meant, but he didn't dare. He was afraid the other boys might laugh at him. It was getting late so Taylor just said good-by, and guess what? He took the FOUR LETTER WORD home with him.

As Taylor walked into the house his mother's cooking reminded him how hungry he was. He was starving and walked straight to the kitchen to watch his mother prepare supper. He waited and waited for dinner to be put on the table, until finally his patience was exhausted and out came the FOUR LETTER WORD. To Taylor's surprise, nothing happened.

"There's nothing to this word," he thought. So he said it again, but this time a little louder. Well, you would have thought the world was coming to an end. Taylor's mother jerked him up, set him on the counter and demanded to know where he had heard such a word.

"The boys in the park," was Taylor's answer. "Everyone says it. What's the big deal?" Taylor asked.

"No, Taylor. Everyone doesn't say it," his mother explained. "You have a choice. People who use such language do stand out. But do you want to stand out in that way?"

Taylor lowered his head and nodded no.

"Didn't you feel a little uncomfortable when you heard it and especially when you said it?" his mother added as she gave him a warm gentle hug. What could Taylor say? He did feel uncomfortable, especially now. With enough said, Taylor's mother promised not to tell his dad and Taylor promised not to use the FOUR LETTER WORD ever again.

THE FOUR LETTER WORD IS A FEABLE EFFORT TO IMPRESS OTHERS, WHEN QUITE OFTEN IT HURTS THE ONES WE LOVE THE M

The next day was Saturday, and Taylor's father had promised to take him fishing. Taylor really enjoyed these special times with his father, so they got up extra early and headed out. He wanted so much to be just like his dad. When they got to the lake, they quickly unloaded their fishing gear and settled down on an old log close to the shore. Before long they were eating pretzels, drinking sodas, and having the time of their lives, even the fish seemed to enjoy their presence as they fought over the bread crumbs Taylor had thrown into the water.

Then it happened, quickly and suddenly, the FOUR LETTER WORD! While casting, Taylor's father got the fish hook stuck in his arm. He opened his mouth to scream, but the FOUR LETTER WORD jumped out. Taylor's father didn't even realize he had said it. This really confused Taylor. The fishing trip was no longer fun, and Taylor just wanted to go home.

The next day Taylor went to his teacher and asked her about the FOUR LETTER WORD. She explained, "Sometimes people use strong words to say how they feel. But once you say a FOUR LETTER WORD you can never take it back. It not only affects you and the person you say it to, but it also affects the other people around you."

She went on, "FOUR LETTER WORDS are nothing more than a habit and can often times determine the kind of friends we have." Taylor thought back on how bad he felt when he heard his father say the FOUR LETTER WORD. He would never want to cause someone else to feel like that.

His teacher's words were powerful and clear, and Taylor couldn't wait to get home and sort all this out with his father. When he got home he sat down with his dad, and they discussed the FOUR LETTER WORD. Much to their surprise, they found a bunch of GOOD FOUR LETTER WORDS: Love, Calm, Lift, Hold, Play, Jest, and Help were just a few of the GOOD FOUR LETTER WORDS they discovered.

From that day forward they both agreed to say only GOOD FOUR LETTER WORDS, and guess what? Even the older boys in the park stopped using the FOUR LETTER WORD around Taylor. They quickly saw that the FOUR LETTER WORD no longer impressed Taylor, and his friendship meant using only GOOD FOUR LETTER WORDS.

DON'T GO NUTS OVER COCONUTS

*A*long, long time ago, way out in the middle of the Pacific Ocean, lived the happiest tribe of monkeys in the world. They once lived on the main island with the rest of the animals, including lions and tigers who found the monkeys to be quite tasty. Then one day several of the monkeys got together and decided to swim to a small island just off the main island. Here they found peace and happiness. There were no lions and no tigers. The monkeys had the whole island to themselves. They were free to play monkey games or just relax on the beach. Whenever they got thirsty or hungry, they just broke open a coconut and drank the sweet milk or ate the tasty meat found inside. What more could a monkey ask for?

The monkeys had found peace and contentment on their small island. Unfortunately, as time went by, they also lost their sense of fear and common sense. They took their paradise for granted.

One warm, lazy summer day a ship came to the island and anchored in the bay. On top of its mast was a flag showing the skull and crossbones. Yes, it was a pirate ship carrying outlaws of the sea. A rough lot these pirates were as they came ashore in their launch boats. Some had patches over their eyes while others were missing arms or legs. By the looks and smell of them, they all needed a long, hot bath.

Even though they were a rough lot, the monkeys gave them little notice. They had seen people come and go before, but they never stayed long or tried to harm any of them. The monkeys would just hang from the tree limbs and enjoy their coconuts until the pirates left.

These men were different, however, they had determination in their eyes. They tried as hard as they could to climb the coconut trees, but failed every time because coconut trees have no lower limbs. Being unable to climb the trees, the pirates gathered around a bonfire and seemed to be drawing something in the sand. Then the most unusual thing happened. They left the bonfire and headed back to the coconut trees. With much effort the pirates picked up a water-soaked log and started pounding the coconut trees as hard as they could, in hopes of dislodging the coconuts.

"What a great game!" thought the monkeys. As the pirates pounded the trees a few coconuts did fall toward the ground but they were quickly grabbed in mid-air

by the monkeys. All the coconuts, except one. This large, hairy coconut just happened to hit one of the pirates right between the eyes as he looked up. A cloud of dirt and dust settled above the pirate as he stumbled about trying to regain his senses. Having failed in their efforts, the pirates returned to their launch boats empty handed and rowed back to the ship in a raw mood.

The monkeys could hear loud and strong talk from the ship well into the night as the pirates argued back and forth. The monkeys assumed they had seen the last of them, but as morning came, so did the pirates. This time they were very serious in their manner. They quickly unloaded and headed straight for the coconut trees. Still the monkeys showed no fear. There was a long silence as the pirates and monkeys just stared at each other.

Then it happened! The meanest, ugliest peg-legged pirate you've ever seen, still sporting a knot between his eyes from yesterday's games, picked up a rock and threw it at the monkeys. "This is strange," thought the monkeys. "What was he trying to prove by throwing a rock at them?"

The rest of the pirates grabbed a handful of rocks and joined in the game to see how many monkeys they could hit. At first the monkeys tried to dodge the rocks and catch the ones that hit them, but even the most patient monkeys were soon angered by the attack.

The anger slowly crept in and took control of them all. In a fit of rage, one of the monkeys pulled a coconut off of his tree and threw it at the pirates, and before long all the monkeys were throwing coconuts. The battle of coconuts and rocks raged on and on until finally the monkeys ran out of coconuts, and the battle ended as quickly as it had begun.

Believing they had won the battle the monkeys cheered and danced as the pirates went back to their launch boats, but to their surprise the pirates returned with big burlap sacks. The monkeys watched as the pirates filled the sacks with all the coconuts they had thrown to the ground. This continued until every single coconut on the island had been gathered up. Once their deed was done the pirates loaded the launch boats with their bounty and headed back to the ship, laughing all the way.

As the ship drifted out to sea, the monkeys slowly came down from the trees. "What have we done?" they thought.

With no coconuts left, they had no choice but to swim back to the main island to live with the lions and tigers. Gone was their paradise. All because they had lost their temper and, in return, they had lost everything.

THE GREATEST GIFT OF ALL

*T*here once was a king who owned all the land and everything in the kingdom. He was a kind and gentle ruler, and the people loved and obeyed his every command.

But one day the Master of the Court advised the king that he would soon have to name an heir to his throne. Having three daughters only made the decision more difficult for the king.

The eldest was the most beautiful woman in all the land. Her name was Elizabeth. Her day was busy with all the necessities to make her beautiful. She visited her dressmaker, the crown jeweler, the hairdresser, and her social secretary every day. The castle was always filled with young men eager to gain her hand in marriage.

The second daughter was Madelon. Madelon was so smart that even the king's wise men dared not dispute her. She loved to read books and spent most of her time in the king's library.

And then there was Grace. She wasn't very beautiful nor was she the smartest in the land. However, the king's court favored her because of her gentle, caring nature. The people of the palace always knew they could come talk to Grace about any problem or thought, and she would listen. She would not always have an answer like Madelon, but she would always make everyone feel better.

One day the king called all three daughters to court and explained that he was going to name one of them as the Royal Princess and heir to the throne. A Royal Decree was then read to the princesses:

"One week from today each of you will be summoned to the court. When you arrive you will be handed a silver tray. Upon that tray you will place a gift for the king and then present it to him. The daughter that offers the greatest gift of all will be named the Royal Princess."

The whole country was excited. What could the daughters possibly carry on a silver platter that would be worthy of the king? The days soon passed, but the daughters dared not talk among themselves for fear that the others might discover what their gift would be.

Finally, the Master of the Court visited the daughters and presented a Royal Summons to each. By this time all the daughters had their gifts except Grace.

Grace went to bed that night still without a gift. As she lay there, she looked into the heavens for guidance, then quite suddenly a warm peace came over Grace, and she drifted off to sleep.

Long lines of people gathered at the palace the next morning. Never had there been so many people at the palace before. Everyone was talking; everyone was curious. With trumpets sounding, the Master of the Court announced the first daughter.

Elizabeth took the silver tray from the Master of the Court and carefully laid a gold box on it. As she walked toward the king everyone wondered what was in the box. Having reached the king, she carefully opened the gold box and took out a rose. Not just any rose, but a black rose. It was as rare and beautiful as Elizabeth. The king smiled and announced, "This is truly a fine gift."

The Master of the Court took the tray and handed it to the second daughter, Madelon. She took a very large book and placed it on the silver tray. Upon reaching the king, he again reached out and in his hand she placed the Book of Wisdom. Madelon knew this book contained all the great thoughts and wisdom of the day. The king again smiled and acknowledged Madelon. "This too is a very fine gift."

Lovingly, Grace received the tray from the Master of the Court and headed toward the king. It was a long walk, and everyone started talking as she got closer because there was nothing on her tray. The people knew she was summoned under a Royal Proclamation and failure to comply meant certain death. As Grace got closer, the king realized the tray was empty.

"How could she do this?" the king thought. "Anything on the tray would save her, but there is nothing." The king was beside himself, what could he do? The law would have to be enforced, even for Grace.

Grace was now before the king and never had the palace been this quiet. She gently placed the empty tray on the floor, took off her shoes, and then stepped inside the tray. Reaching up, she hugged the king, and said, "Father, all I have to offer you is myself. I know of no greater gift than my love and devotion to you." The king stepped back in amazement. Truly this was the greatest gift. Instantly the king announced Grace as the Royal Princess.

PIER PRESSURE

*T*ully came from a long line of famous tugboats. His grandfather was the first tugboat to be built in the harbor, and his father, being the mightiest and strongest tugboat in the area, was given the honor of pulling the big cruise ships loaded with anxious tourists into the bay.

Every day Tully went out to sea to grab hold of rusty old barges and pull them into port—BIG DEAL! What he really wanted to be was a speed boat. They were fast and free to go anywhere they wanted, not slow and tied to a rope most of the time like he was. Tully also dreamed of being a big, stately cruise ship. The stories they could tell of far off places would cause any boat to toot his horn.

Tully thought his life would always be dull and uneventful. Little did he know that on this particular night an event would change his life forever. A terrible hurricane was quickly closing in on the harbor. Never had anyone seen such powerful winds, rain, and waves. The storm damaged or destroyed every boat in the harbor, all except for Tully.

Tully slept safe and secure each night in his special windproof boathouse. This strongest of boathouses was built for Tully's father in gratitude for his many years of service in the harbor. Now it was Tully's turn to serve, and his father had given the boathouse to him. Tully had worked his way up the tugboat line, yet still had not achieved the confidence to pull the ocean liners and other grand ships of the sea.

The morning after the storm everything was in a state of panic and confusion. The harbor master had received a "MAY DAY" from a cruise ship far out in the ocean. "We have a ship full of people and we are sinking fast!" the cruise ship captain shouted into the radio. In an effort to try and save the sinking ship, the harbor master looked up and down the docks hoping to find a boat that was not too damaged by the storm. None could be found, but then he remembered Tully's windproof boathouse.

The harbor master quickly woke Tully and explained the situation to him. As Tully listened he was calm on the outside, while terrified on the inside. "I've never been that far out into the ocean," he thought. "And I've never even pulled an ocean liner. What if I can't?" Tully reached deep inside himself and grabbed all the courage he could, and with a deep breath, he said, "Yes, I will do it."

There was no time to waste. Tully filled his tanks with gas and headed out to sea. As he left the harbor his courage began to slip; however, he remembered the words of encouragement his grandfather always told him when he was down. "No matter what the job, do your very best. We are all capable of doing far more than we ever think we can. So when things get tough, reach deep inside—that's where you will find the strength to carry you through."

With his courage renewed, Tully continued on until he reached the sinking ship. And what a ship it was! Tully had never seen a ship of this size, how would he ever pull this monster to safety? Remembering what his grandfather had told him, he pulled alongside the ship, and tied his ropes to her giving a mighty pull, but nothing happened. The ship did not move at all.

Tully had spent his whole life tugging old rusty barges so he wouldn't fail and disappoint all those who knew him. "How would he ever weather this storm?" he thought.

A twenty-foot high tidal wave had torn a big hole in the side of the ship. Tully overheard the ship's captain say that the ship's hull was filling up with water and they would soon sink to the bottom of the ocean. The weight of the water inside the cruise ship was too much for Tully to handle. What was he to do?

Remembering a story his grandfather had told him, Tully eased up to the hole on the side of the ship and plugged it with his side. Now Tully was like a big Band-Aid. He had never realized just how important his grandfather's stories would be until this moment when he needed them the most.

When the captain saw what Tully was doing, he quickly ordered the crew to start the water pumps. It wasn't long before most of the water had been pumped out, and the ship was lighter and floating on top of the water. Tully was able to pull the ship home now.

When Tully and the cruise ship came into the harbor the band was playing, and all the people were shouting praises to Tully. To them he was not just another old rusty tugboat—he was special! Tully had allowed himself to take that extra step to go beyond what was expected. And you know what? Tully now understood that all boats are special, even little rusty tugboats.

CHANGE FOR A BUCKY

*H*ave you ever wished you were stronger, faster, or perhaps smarter than you really are? Bucky thought being bigger and stronger would make him better than everyone else, and perhaps more popular. Let's see what happens to Bucky as he learns a very valuable lesson.

Bucky and his two best friends, Joe and Al, played football on the playground every afternoon after school. There wasn't anything special about the three boys. I guess that's why they were such good friends. They would play for hours taking turns being the leader.

Bucky was the kind of boy who wouldn't hurt a fly. In fact, he would be the first to say "I'm sorry" whenever something happened, even if it wasn't his fault. Can you see why the other boys liked Bucky?

It was getting late one day and the boys were tired from playing football, so they headed home. Bucky decided to take the shortcut through the alley, even though his mother had told him several times not to go that way. He knew he was taking a chance, since The Messengers, the gang of all gangs, hung out in the alley sometimes.

"What do mothers know? Besides, I can take care of myself," thought Bucky. Well guess who Bucky ran into while walking through the alley? The Messengers. At first they just teased him, but then it got serious. They bullied him, hit him, and then stole his football. They ran off calling him "Bucky the Wimp".

The days passed, but Bucky just couldn't seem to forget what had happened. One morning while Bucky was eating his cereal, he saw an ad in his dad's newspaper. The ad read: "DON'T BE A WIMP: I Can Make You Confident, Strong, and the Most Popular Kid in School. Mail Today." Well, that's just what Bucky did, and every day he would check the mailbox to see if his special book had arrived. The waiting was tough. Then one day the package finally arrived. "All of my problems will be solved," he shouted.

The book taught Bucky how important it was to exercise and eat the right kinds of foods. Bucky followed the book's advice carefully and he slowly started to gain weight and big muscles. Of course, we all know that eating right and exercising are good for us. As the weeks passed, Bucky's body slowly started to change and so did his attitude. He was not the considerate, thoughtful little boy he had been.

Instead of being part of the team, Bucky now wanted to be in charge of the team. At first his best friends, Joe and Al, went along with Bucky, but before too long they stopped asking Bucky to play with them. With his new attitude, Bucky felt the breakup of their friendship was Al and Joe's loss, not his. As he lost his old friends, he gained new ones. Can you guess who became Bucky's new friends?

One day after school Bucky ran into the Messengers. They started teasing him again, but this time Bucky was ready for them. He went straight for the leader of the gang. This was not the Bucky they had known. Instead of fighting with Bucky, the gang asked him to join them. Bucky had just the right attitude they were looking for. By joining the gang, Bucky felt important and better than the other kids at school.

It did not take Bucky long to start thinking and acting like the other gang members. Bucky was popular, but popular with all the wrong people. The tougher he got, the tougher the other gang members expected him to be. This was not what Bucky wanted, but these were the only friends he had now.

One day Bucky and the other gang members were hanging out in the alley when Joe and Al came walking by. At first the gang started teasing Joe and Al by knocking off their hats and calling them sissy names, but then they started pushing and punching the boys.

"Is this what I have become? A bully to my friends," Bucky thought to himself. "All I wanted was to be popular. What a mess I have made of things." He was tired of this phony life and quickly pushed through the gang members, "Joe...Al...I'm sorry for this treatment. Go on home. They won't hurt you anymore." As Joe and Al ran down the alley they could see the punches that were meant for them being aimed at Bucky.

Because of his actions, the Messengers abandoned Bucky as quickly as they had accepted him. He no longer served their needs and now he was really alone. As he walked home, all he could think about was how much Al and Joe's friendship had meant to him.

Bucky learned a very valuable lesson that day. As his body changed and grew stronger and bigger, he learned that his heart needed to grow in love, not hate. Strength of character comes not from being better than others but from caring about others. It took a while for his old friends to accept him back, but in time they did. Bucky just likes being Bucky; only now he is a little stronger, a lot bigger and much wiser.

THE FLEA BARGAIN

$\mathcal{C}$hucky was a woodchuck with an attitude—an attitude of always asking, "Why? Why do the seasons change? Why do some animals dig holes and live in the ground while others climb and live in trees? Why? Why? Why?" Most of the other woodchucks made fun of Chucky and considered him a pest, but that didn't stop Chucky. He still wanted to know...why?

One bright spring morning, Chucky came out of his den, sat up on his haunches, and noticed that every woodchuck he could see was scratching. "Fleas, fleas, fleas—they will drive you crazy," Chucky thought. Of course, Chucky asked, "Why? Why are fleas such a problem?"

No one seemed to have an answer, so Chucky went to the Council of Elders, the wise, old woodchucks who carried out the law of the land, as far as woodchucks were concerned. Their response was, "Fleas have always been a part of our lives and always will be. That's just the way it is and you cannot change some things in life."

"Nonsense," thought Chucky. "I will find a way to get rid of my fleas."

First he tried running as fast as he could, hoping to shake them off. All this did was to shake them up and make them biting mad. He then tried rubbing up against a pine tree, thinking the pine sap would run them off. Boy, did the other woodchucks laugh at Chucky when he came back all sticky and smelling like a pine tree.

Determined to succeed, Chucky then went inside a cave and built a big smoky fire. As he sat in the cave, his eyes began to water and his lungs began to burn. "Surely the fleas must be hurting as bad as I am," he thought. Only the smokier it got, the deeper the fleas buried themselves into his fur.

Finally, he buried himself in mud. He just knew this would drive the fleas away. The only thing it drove away were the few friends Chucky had left.

Well, Chucky finally gave up. The elders were right. Fleas would always be a part of a woodchuck's life, and the other woodchucks continued to tease Chucky. "Hey, Chucky have you seen any fleas lately? Chucky, have you had your mud bath today?" His friends' cruel teasing hurt Chucky's feelings.

One day Chucky's mother explained, "Chucky, you have a wonderful imagination. Don't be discouraged. Because you ask questions and try to find the answers,

THE MORE TIME YOU SPEND IMPROVING YOURSELF, THE LESS TIME YOU HAVE TO WORRY ABOUT WHAT OTHERS SAY ABOUT YOU.

you will make a difference in this world. Dream your dreams and never stop asking why." His mother gave him new confidence. He felt better now and would not be discouraged by his friends' ridicule.

The next day Chucky went to the creek, bent over, and started sipping the cool spring water. As his front feet touched the water, he noticed that the fleas moved up his legs to avoid the water. "That's it!" he shouted as he jumped with excitement. "The fleas don't like water."

Chucky slowly and very carefully stepped further into the creek. Sure enough, the fleas continued to move up his legs and then up his body to his head until his head was the only part of his body above water. Chucky took a deep breath and slowly lowered his head underwater. He just knew all the fleas would jump off the end of his nose by the time he came up for air. But when he came up, the fleas came up, too. They had also held their breath. By the time Chucky got back to the creek bank, his body was still covered with fleas. Only this time, they were really mad. Oh, how the biting made his life miserable.

Thank goodness, Chucky did not stop trying, even though most woodchucks would have. He was determined to find the right approach to getting rid of the fleas forever, despite his failure and despite the ridicule of his friends.

After the fleas finally settled down, Chucky went over to an old oak tree that had fallen, and sat down to think. "Let's see, I can get the fleas all the way to the end of my nose, but no further." Suddenly Chucky noticed one of his fleas jump off, land on one of the fallen oak tree branches, and then quickly disappear.

All of a sudden he knew what to do. Chucky picked up a branch of that old oak tree, put it in his mouth, and headed back to the creek. As he stepped into the water, once again the fleas moved up Chucky's body as the water got deeper. This time, however, when the fleas got to Chucky's head and then his nose, they continued right onto the tree branch that was held securely in his mouth. When the last flea got on board, Chucky let go of the branch, and the fleas slowly drifted away. Because of Chucky's Flea Bargain, the woodchucks were now free of fleas at last.

Before long all the fleas in the forest soon learned to avoid woodchucks, because no woodchuck was worth a trip down the rapids.

The other woodchucks never laughed at Chucky's efforts to make things better again. Chucky helped them realize that failure should not be looked upon as an end, but as a means to an end.

JAY BEE'S TRASH

*J*ay Bee was one of those fellows everybody liked. Because Jay Bee liked himself, he was able to like others, and they, in turn, liked Jay Bee. Sounds confusing, doesn't it? But it's not. Before someone else can like you, you must first like yourself.

Jay Bee was the best bus driver in the city. He was never late and knew all his regular riders by their first names. He always wore a smile and always had something nice to say to each person as they got on the bus.

Then one day Jay Bee found a note taped to his seat on the bus. Although the note was full of praise, its intent was clear. The city was changing and the route Jay Bee had grown to love was being shut down. His new schedule took him through the worst parts of town, and Jay Bee was not a happy bus driver.

The new route also required him to stop and wait for 30 minutes every day for a local factory to let out. Although he was not one who liked to just sit and do nothing, Jay Bee had no choice. However, he was determined to do his best.

On the first day of his new route, Jay Bee put on his best uniform and headed to work as usual. Only this time when he cranked up his bus to leave the station, he turned left instead of right. His mind raced through the last twenty years and wondered what the next twenty years would be like.

He greeted each new rider with a smile and a friendly hello, just like before, and to his surprise Jay Bee found he liked meeting his new riders, and the new route wasn't nearly as bad as he thought it would be.

As the day was coming to an end, he knew he had one more stop to make—his 30-minute stopover—but he was prepared. With book in hand, he pulled over to the bus stop and quickly found himself in the country, reading about life on a farm.

Jay Bee loved to read, but the traffic noise kept disturbing him, and every time he looked up he saw the ugly, vacant lot across from the factory, full of trash and unwanted items. Finally, he couldn't stand it any longer. Jay Bee grabbed the little trash bag next to his seat and jumped off the bus to pick up trash on that old vacant lot.

Well, it didn't take long for him to fill the little trash bag, but he felt better.

As Jay Bee was driving home from work that day he noticed a lot of ugly vacant

lots along the way. His city was dying, but what could one person do? Fine state-ly buildings, rich in history towered over the vacant lots, only now most of them were boarded up and covered with spray paint. Jay Bee thought to himself, "What a waste. Surely something can be done to bring this part of town back to life."

The next day Jay Bee returned to the vacant lot with a whole box of large trash bags, and every day for a week he spent that 30 minutes picking up trash. By the end of the week, the whole neighborhood started noticing what Jay Bee was doing, and one by one they started coming over to help him clean up the lot. Before long the lot was clean as a whistle, something for the whole neighborhood to be proud of.

After all the trash and junkyard debris were picked up, Jay Bee started noticing that the whole neighborhood was looking better. Windows were being washed, flower pots were popping up on window sills, and the smell of fresh paint filled the air. The neighborhood was coming back to life. And to think it all started with one person picking up one piece of trash!

With the lot clean and the neighborhood looking better, Jay Bee settled into reading about life on the farm, and his 30-minute stopovers became his favorite time of the day. One day while Jay Bee was reading about the joy of growing your own carrots, Mrs. Bitterhoney came on the bus, just a-fussing.

"What's the point of cleaning up that old vacant lot if you don't do anything with it," she shouted.

"Ms. Bitterhoney is right," Jay Bee thought. Then he remembered his garden-ing books and replied, "Why don't we plant a garden?"

"A garden? Why, you can't plant a garden in the city," Mrs. Bitterhoney shout-ed. "That's ridiculous!" she mumbled as she took her usual seat on the second row. Jay Bee looked in his mirror and gave her a big smile anyway, because she had given him a splendid idea.

Ridiculous or not, Jay Bee decided to check it out. Before the end of the week, Jay Bee had gotten permission from the owner of the lot to plant a garden. He held a meeting for the entire neighborhood and, each person who had helped clean up the lot was given a plot to call his own. Well, never had there been such excitement in the neighborhood. The new gardeners formed a garden club, and everybody got to know each other just like neighbors should.

By the end of the summer, there wasn't a vacant lot left in the entire city. Beautiful gardens were everywhere, and it all started because one person picked up one piece of trash.

OUT ON A LIMB

*D*o you know where the first Christmas trees came from? The Christmas tree tradition began far, far away across the ocean in a country named Germany. Deep in the dark woods of the Black Forest there stood a stand of Christmas trees which no man had ever seen. In the middle of this stand was a little fir tree whose only ambition in life was to become the tallest and proudest Christmas tree in the woods.

The little tree was surrounded by tall, stately Christmas trees, and he was proud to be among them. What he didn't like, however, was their constant attention. In other words, they were always telling him what to do, or so he thought.

"I'm going to mind my own business and not be bossy, even when I'm 200 years old. Yes, indeed, that's what I'll do," he reflected.

One evening the North Wind blew its cold breathe upon the forest to alert all creatures of the approaching ice and snow storms. The tall trees cautioned the little Christmas tree, "You need to cover your roots with a blanket of leaves, little one; otherwise, this winter could be your last."

The little tree angrily brushed his limbs back and forth and replied, "Winter is at least another week away and I have got plenty of time to protect my roots."

After the little tree refused their advice, the tall trees started pushing some leaves around his trunk but the little Christmas tree was defiant and pushed the leaves away. "When I need your advice I'll ask for it, after all I'm just as smart as you are."

"Okay," said the big trees, "but don't say we didn't warn you, especially when all your limbs fall to the ground and the termites make quick work of your future."

As night fell the little tree was safe and warm and proud of his decision. "Just wait until morning," he thought, "the tall trees will see that I was right."

As the night went on, the little tree started getting colder and colder, and ice started forming on his branches. In fact, his branches became so stiff with ice that he could not shake his limbs at all. It was too late now. He could not cover his roots with a soft protective layer of leaves, and by morning his roots would be frozen.

When the first light of day peeped over the mountain top, the tall Christmas trees looked down and saw that the little tree was frozen, and in great danger of dying. As the sun continued to rise, the big trees moved their branches away so the

little tree could get as much sunlight as possible. They covered his roots with a thick warm layer of leaves, but even with all their help, it took three days for the little tree to thaw out.

"Is he going to live?" they all asked.

Finally at the end of the third day, the little tree was able to move his branches, however, he was very weak and too ashamed to talk to the other trees. As the days went on, the little Christmas tree started losing his branches. One by one they fell to the ground. There was nothing he could do to stop it. By the end of winter, he had only two limbs left, and they were hanging pretty low to the ground. He was no longer a beautiful little Christmas tree.

By this time the big trees hoped he had learned his lesson, but they waited until the little tree wanted their advice and help. Until he softened his attitude and willingly accepted the tall trees' advice, their words of wisdom would still fall on deaf limbs.

The little tree finally realized that if he lost his last two limbs he would surely die. The little Christmas tree was no longer a proud, defiant upstart. He swallowed his pride and asked, "Please tell me what to do? I don't want to die."

The tall trees lovingly bent down and showed him that they still cared. "Listen closely," they said. "Every day you must lift your remaining branches up to the sun. Then dig your roots deep into the soil and drink as much water as possible. And finally you have to stand very still in the evening so that your wounds will heal."

There was no argument this time. The little tree did exactly as they said. Ever so slowly, the wounds began to heal, and new branches started popping out everywhere. The little tree was going to live.

Deep in the dark woods of the Black Forest there still remains a stand of Christmas trees which no man has ever seen. In the middle of this stand is the tallest, proudest tree of them all. However, if you look closely at this majestic fir tree you will see the scars made by a defiant, little Christmas tree. The beautiful tree wears his scars proudly because they remind him to always accept the advice of others as graciously and lovingly as it is given.

It took the now stately, tall Christmas tree a hundred years to recover from his defiance. The next hundred years were going to be different. He would spend the rest of his life bending down and offering advice to defiant young upstarts, just as the tall trees had done for him.

WORRIED PINK

*S*ara was no different than you and I. She loved being the center of attention. However, sometimes we all make bad decisions in the effort to be liked.

"Today was just awful. Mary is having a birthday party after school, and she didn't invite me." This distressing thought was all Sara could think about as she dragged herself home from school. She went straight to her room and cried herself to sleep.

After supper, while her mother was washing the dishes, Sara got out her mother's jewelry box and lost herself in all the many different kinds of jewelry she found. Off to itself was a gold and velvet box which Sara knew had to be special. Inside Sara found the most beautiful ring she had ever seen. It was gold with a large pink stone in the center surrounded by little pink stones. "Boy, would the girls at school be impressed if she could wear such a ring to school," Sara thought.

The next morning, Sara tucked her mother's ring into her pocket and headed to school. As soon as her house was out of sight, Sara placed the ring on her finger. She could just visualize her friends talking about the ring all day. Why, she would be queen for a day. What Sara didn't realize was that if someone was impressed by only outward appearances and not for herself, then they were probably not worth knowing.

Sure enough, the girls who were impressed by the ring quickly showed signs of jealously and started to make fun of Sara, while her friends didn't let the ring affect their attitude toward her at all. By lunch time Sara realized that taking the ring was a big mistake, and understood that one's true value came from what's on the inside, not the outside.

Sara quickly forgot about the ring, and joined some friends for a game of hopscotch on the playground. Soon the bell sounded, and it was time to return to class. Sara sat down, took out her pencil and notebook, and then realized her mother's ring was not on her finger. She felt numb all over and could scarcely breathe, was she in a pickle now. After school Sara spent two hours looking for her mother's ring. It had to be on the playground, but where? She finally realized it was hopeless and gave up.

Mr. Carter, her science teacher, was leaving school when he saw Sara. As they

TO BE ACCEPTED AS YOU ARE, YOU MUST FIRST BE WILLING TO ACCEPT OTHERS AS THEY ARE

walked down the steps, he noticed how sad Sara looked. Sara did not like Mr. Carter. She thought he was mean, hard, and unfair as a teacher. These feelings came mainly because Sara didn't like science, and her grades reflected that attitude. Sara finally explained to Mr. Carter what had happened. "What shall I do?" Sara asked. "My mother will be so angry with me."

Mr. Carter softly explained that there was only one thing to do. "Just be honest, don't lie, and really be sorry for what you have done."

"That sounds easy, but you don't know my mother," Sara replied. However, Sara did take Mr. Carter's advice. When she got home, she poured her heart out to her mother. "Are you angry?" Sara asked.

"I'm hurt and upset," her mother replied. "That ring was the only treasure my mother left me when she died. Your grandmother said one day I would know the true value of the ring. Now I will never know what she meant."

Sara's tears poured down her cheeks as her mother continued, "Trust is something that is lost in an instant and may take months or years to earn back. I hope you have learned not to take something that is not yours." Sara nodded and was glad when her mother hugged her. "I love you more than any old ring," she added, "and I am so proud that you were honest with me. But you will have to be punished for taking the ring without my permission."

The punishment would be easy. The worst part was thinking that her mother might not ever love her again. She learned that a mother's love is unconditional. Her mother would always love her and take care of her. Even though she had made a wrong choice, her mother would be there to help guide her.

Early the next morning Mr. Carter drove up to Sara's house, jumped out of his car, and ran toward the house shouting, "I've found it! I've found the ring!" The family quickly gathered around him, and they all shared his joy. Mr. Carter had been up most of the night looking for the ring with a metal detector. He asked, "Why is such a valuable ring not locked up in a safe?"

"I don't understand what you mean, Mr. Carter. It's only a gemstone ring my mother left me when she died," Sara's mother replied.

"Only a gemstone!" Mr. Carter shouted. "My dear, these pink stones are pink diamonds which are the rarest of all diamonds and worth a small fortune."

Now they all knew the value of the ring in dollars, but Sara's honesty and her mother's forgiveness were much more valuable and could not be measured in dollars; they had a treasure which could only be found when love is placed first and diamonds second.

TO ACCEPT HOW YOU LOOK ON THE OUTSIDE CAN BE THE FIRST STEP TO ACCEPTING HOW YOU FEEL ON THE INSIDE.

LIMBARK'S FREE RIDE

*H*ave you ever met an unhappy squirrel? Probably not, because squirrels are almost always happy. They just seem to play all day while jumping from tree to tree without a care in the world. Then there was Limbark who never seemed to be happy. If he had one nut, he wanted two nuts; if he got to be the leader one day, he wanted to be the leader every day. As time went by, fewer and fewer squirrels would play with Limbark because he was too hard to please.

One day while playing alone he got the idea to cut his hair down to the soft, white undercoat. He was tired of looking like all the other squirrels in the trees. Without all that fur, he would be cooler and combing his hair would be a breeze. Limbark got his mother's scissors from her sewing chest and went to work cutting his hair. As he made the final snips he looked in the mirror and said, "Yes, I look great." Limbark was no longer brown but white and fluffy. He was cool looking and cool feeling, just what he wanted.

As Limbark sat down for dinner Mr. and Mrs. Squirrel gasped in horror. "Son, what have your done?" Mr. Squirrel shouted. "Don't you realize that your brown fur allows you to hide in the trees? Now you have no natural protection. So please be very careful when you leave the house," his father added. But Limbark was so proud of himself that his father's words of wisdom were quickly forgotten.

For several days Limbark played in the trees with the comfort of knowing he had done the right thing. The other squirrels warned him to stay close to his family tree. But Limbark decided he could take care of himself without their advice, so off he scampered to the big walnut tree in the meadow. Suddenly without warning, he felt sharp needles in his back, and the next thing he knew he was flying in the air. He looked up and realized that an eagle had him in his claws. Well, there was nothing he could do but go along for the ride.

When Mr. Eagle landed he hurried in to show Mrs. Eagle what he had brought home for supper. Mrs. Eagle looked at Limbark and shouted, "What a strange looking squirrel. He doesn't have any hair except for his undercoat."

Mr. Eagle explained, "That's why he was so easy to see in the walnut tree. All squirrels should be this color."

As the oven was getting hot, Mrs. Eagle examined Limbark very carefully. "Perhaps he has a terrible disease," she cried.

"No way," said Mr. Eagle, as he checked to see if the oven was hot enough.

"I will not cook this squirrel," declared Mrs. Eagle. "He's too sickly."

"If you don't, I will," shouted Mr. Eagle with a determined look in his eye.

By this time, Limbark was so scared that he started to tremble. "I told you this squirrel was sick. Look at him," yelled Mrs. Eagle, and she threw Limbark out the window. Mr. Eagle took off after Limbark, but the little squirrel managed to get away under the dark blanket of night.

That night was the worst night of his life. Limbark was all alone and scared, and only after the sun came up did he stop shaking. He could still feel the eagle's claws in his back as he kept a careful lookout for Mr. Eagle and his sharp eagle eyes. Limbark could still hear Mrs. Eagle's oven door squeak as she would check to see if it was hot enough yet.

Mr. Eagle had taken Limbark to the mountains...a far trek from squirrel valley. "Will I ever find my way home?" Limbark thought. He was still white and on eagle mountain, so Limbark was going to have to be very careful.

For three nights Limbark searched for his home, while by day he would lie under the bushes for fear of being spotted again by Mr. Eagle. During these idle hours he would watch the other squirrels play and have fun. Only when darkness came and the forest became silent did Limbark dare venture out into the open. He was scared and lonely, and hours seemed like days. Finally, on the third night, just as the dawn was starting to awaken the forest, Limbark spotted the familiar tree where his home was.

He raced up the tree as fast as he could, hoping his parents still loved him. With open arms, they welcomed him back. They were so glad to see him.

"Where have you been? We have been so worried," his parents stated.

Limbark told them of his high flying ride to the mountain top, and his narrow escape from the eagles' oven. Then he added, "Mom, can you go down to the river with me and rub brown mud all over me? I really don't want to be white anymore." They all laughed and were happy to have their little brown squirrel back.

Limbark is a lot like you and me. We all use our imagination and creativity to be different and change things. Just be sure to think through the consequences of your actions or you might end up taking a free ride to places you had rather not go.

THE GENTLEST MATADOR

Just imagine getting paid to play with your favorite pets all day. Well, Carlos had just such a job, except most people didn't consider his pets to be pets at all. The meanest, most ferocious bulls in all of Mexico were Carlos' responsibility to feed and water every day.

Carlos was a hard worker for a young boy. Every afternoon he would go to the training stables and care for the bulls. He was sad, however, because the bulls were trained to be so mean. People wanted and expected bulls to be mean, so they could be used in the popular bullfights.

At first the bulls charged Carlos whenever he approached them. They did not understand kindness and friendship, no matter how hard Carlos tried. Carlos' mother always told him, "Kind words can tame the wildest beasts. Just remember, Carlos, it is hard to hate someone when all they speak are kind words."

So Carlos kept trying. He spoke softly and kindly, even to the meanest bulls on the ranch. Over and over again he would say, "I just want to be your friend," and ever so slowly the bulls started liking Carlos. He even had names for some of the bulls. His favorite was Merango, the biggest bull in the stable.

One day there was a great fire which destroyed the stables. All the bulls were sold, and Carlos no longer had a job. His family needed money, so he decided to go into the big city and look for work. The trip was long and hard. Carlos had never journeyed so far from home before, and oh, how he missed his family and his bulls.

The city was scary to Carlos. It was big and noisy, and he was all alone. Carlos had no city skills and was unable to find any work, but he remembered his father telling him about the great bullfights. Perhaps, he could help care for the bulls. "That's it, that's it," he shouted as he hurried to the great arena where the bullfights take place.

The manager of the arena quickly pointed out to Carlos that the bulls are brought in the day of the bullfights. "The longer and hotter the ride, the meaner the bulls are," he declared. "The only care the bulls need the day of the bullfight is no care," the manager went on to say. "If you really need a job we could use a new, young matador. This is all I have to offer you," the manager replied.

"A matador hurts the bulls with spears and such," thought Carlos. "I could

never do that." But his family was depending on him, so Carlos agreed to take the position of matador, and word quickly spread that a new, young matador was in town.

Carlos practiced as hard as he could to be a matador, but his heart just wasn't in it. The bulls were his friends. How could he kill something he loved so much.

As time approached for him to enter the arena, he tried on his matador suit, he had to admit, he looked pretty good. Maybe it would be fun to be a matador. The suit made him feel different and the sounds of the crowd in the arena started his adrenaline running. He knew this was going to be a very special day in his life.

The next bullfight was packed with people shouting praises to Carlos, the new, young matador. As the manager pushed Carlos into the arena, the crowd went crazy and started throwing roses and shouting, "Carlos! Carlos! Carlos!" Then it happened. The crowd noise came to a sudden halt, the gates opened, and there he was—the biggest, meanest bull you have ever seen. Boy, was he mad! His nostrils flared and snorted as he charged barrels, clowns, and anything else he saw. Then the arena was cleared and only Carlos and the bull remained.

Carlos opened his red cape out to his side as the bull charged toward him with fire in his eyes. As the bull was about to tear into Carlos, he lowered his cape and looked the bull straight in the eye and softly said, "I just want to be your friend." All of a sudden the raging bull stopped dead in his tracks. Carlos opened his arms and gave the bull a big hug. It was Merango, Carlos' bull. Never had the crowd seen such a sight: a matador petting a bull.

At first the crowd booed. They came to a bullfight not a petting zoo, and they wanted to see a fight. Then slowly they started to cheer as they realized that Carlos had tamed the wildest of bulls with only words. As Carlos and Merango bowed, the crowd showered them with roses and money. So much money, in fact, that Carlos had enough to buy Merango, and the burned down ranch where he had worked.

Carlos restored the ranch and turned it into a retirement home for raging bulls. He now spends his days changing the raging, hate-filled bulls into warm, loving animals. Soft words and kindness still tame the wildest beasts, and his pasture land was now a graceland.

BLACKIE, LOOSE LIPS & GREEN EYES

Once upon a time there were three ducks. They could swim, fly, and do all the things ducks are supposed to do, however, each was special in his own way. In fact, that's why they were named Blackie, Loose Lips, and Green Eyes.

Blackie was pitch black in color; in fact he was so black, he would just disappear into the night. Whenever the ducks got together and had a quack-up, it was easy to spot Blackie because all the other ducks were white.

Green Eyes, as you might have already guessed, had green eyes. No big deal, except all the other ducks had brown eyes. His ability to see better at night because of his green eyes seemed of little value to the other ducks. The only thing they wanted to do at night was to sleep.

Lastly, there was Loose Lips. No, her lips were not loose; they just didn't fit together very well. Every time she closed her mouth there was a gap between the upper and lower bill. Whenever she quacked everyone noticed because her crooked bill gave her the most unusual sound.

The ducks loved their home in the marsh except during duck hunting season. That was the fearful time of the year when no duck was safe. Because ducks are white, the hunters loved to hunt them at dusk. They would come in with their dogs just as the sun was setting. The dogs would find the ducks and scare them so bad they would fly right into the hunters' sights. A white duck against a black sky made an easy target for the hunters. Every year there were fewer ducks while the number of hunters seemed to grow larger.

One day the head quacker called a meeting of all the ducks. "Something has to be done," he declared. There was talk of leaving the marsh and heading further North, but it would be hard to leave their home.

"This is our home; what are we to do? one of the duck's quacked.

"I think we should bury our heads in the sand. If we don't hear the dogs coming we are less likely to quack up and fly into harm's way," another suggested.

Then Blackie spoke up. "Why don't I fly overhead at night and when I see the dogs coming, I can fly back and warn everyone?" The ducks were excited, it was indeed a good plan.

Sure enough, that night the hunters returned to the marsh as usual. Blackie

CHARACTER IS NOT SOMETHING YOU'RE BORN WITH, IT'S SOMETHING YOU SPEND A LIFETIME BUILDING.

took off, knowing his black color would hide him against the dark sky. He soon found the hunters' dogs and they were headed straight for the other ducks. Blackie quickly flew back to warn the others, but by the time everyone had gathered around, it was too late. The dogs were already scattering the ducks, and once again the hunters were having a fine day at the ducks' expense.

The next day the ducks had another meeting. Realizing that timing was everything, Loose Lips suggested, "I can hide up in the old Cypress tree. When Blackie spots the dogs, he can fly over to me and I will give my special call warning everyone to move away from the area." Because Loose Lips had such an unusual quack, everyone was sure to hear the signal. This was even a better plan.

That night everything worked just as Loose Lips had hoped. When Blackie spotted the dogs, he quickly found Loose Lips, and she, in turn, warned the ducks that danger was near. The ducks were saved...or were they? In their panic to flee, they all scattered and flew into each other causing quite a stir. The hunters were quick to head toward the confusion.

"What are we to do?" the ducks cried out the next day and panic quickly spread among the flock. Green Eyes spoke up and said, "My green eyes allow me to see quite well at night. I will be glad to lead the flock to safety." After much discussion they all agreed to follow Green Eyes in an orderly manner when they heard Loose Lips' signal.

Sure enough, the next night more hunters and dogs invaded their marsh. Blackie quickly spotted the dogs and signaled Loose Lips to sound off. Green Eyes then led the entire flock to safety, and not a single duck was lost that night. Before long, word spread that there were no more ducks in the marsh and the hunters headed to more fertile hunting grounds.

Blackie, Loose Lips and Green Eyes were heroes. The flock gave a big party and all three ducks were given the Grand Quacker Medal of Honor. The head quacker presented each duck with his metal and stated, "There's not a duck in our flock that doesn't have special talents and abilities. However, if they are not used they are worthless. Blackie, Green Eyes and Loose Lips recognized their special abilities and used them to save the flock. We are proud and forever thankful that the three of you had the courage to quack up."

BUBBLES

Mary Ann was just about the saddest little girl in her school. She didn't have a lot of friends, she wasn't very pretty, she didn't make good grades, and her home life was the pits. Her parents didn't understand her, and her little brother was always getting in the way.

One night while she was lying in bed half-asleep, she heard a tapping on her window. There, to her surprise, was the ugliest, the greenest, the most bug-eyed frog she had ever seen. At first Mary Ann ignored the frog's tapping. Soon the taps became irritating, so she opened the window and asked the frog, "What do you want?"

"Why, I'm your magic frog, Bubbles," the frog replied. "I'm here on a special assignment, just for you. What can I do to help you?"

Of course, Mary Ann did not believe him. But she did not meet talking frogs every day, so she decided to let him come inside for the night.

Once inside, Bubbles settled down and again asked, "What can I do to help you?"

"Help, you can't help me," Mary Ann replied. "You're a frog. The only thing you are good for is croaking and fried frog legs."

Well, fried frog legs were not what Bubbles had in mind, so he hopped over to an inviting soft slipper in the corner and settled down for the evening. Strange were his last words for the night, "Let the magic begin."

First thing the next morning, Mary Ann's little brother woke her up by pulling her hair with his sticky, dirty fingers. Bubbles quickly hopped over to Mary Ann and whispered, "Your little brother loves you and wants your attention. Instead of shouting and hitting him, why don't you wash his hands and play with him in bed? If you're nice to him, you will be surprised what magic can happen."

Reluctantly, she tried Bubble's suggestion and to her surprise, her brother was really a lot of fun. So Mary Ann started spending more time playing with her brother instead of fighting with him. Her parents soon noticed the change. Because Mary Ann was more loving and understanding with her brother, her parents became more loving and understanding with her.

Bubbles also had some advice on Mary Ann's appearance. Every morning she wore the same old jeans and a T-shirt to school. She half-combed her hair and

always wore a frown on her face. Bubbles jumped up on her vanity and said, "Mary Ann, you would look so nice in that pretty new jumper your mom bought. She cares about you and knows how pretty you would look in this color, and with your hair combed back with a big red ribbon, you will be surprised what will happen. That frown will magically turn into a smile, and since smiles are contagious, it will be very hard for others not to smile back."

Well, Mary Ann did as Bubbles suggested, and to her surprise, the school hours passed so quickly that she could hardly wait to go back the next day. For the first time, the other children in school wanted to be around Mary Ann. Her smile and her appearance caused other children to feel good, too. Mary Ann was beginning to see that Bubbles really was a magical frog.

After softball practice that afternoon, Mary Ann was headed for the television set to slowly slide into dullness. Bubbles eased up to her side with her math book and said, "That math test will be a breeze tomorrow if we review some of the problems this afternoon. I sure would like to see your mom and dad's faces when they see what a good job you can do at school."

Mary Ann thought about it and everything Bubbles had said up to that point had magically come true, so she went to her room and studied for her math test. The next day she came home proudly announcing, "Mom, I made the highest score in my class. I never thought I was good at math but I guess I just never tried," she added.

"I am so proud of you. I have been noticing that you have improved your appearance, your attitude and now your grades. I guess my little girl is growing up to be a responsible young lady. I can't wait to tell your father."

That night Mary Ann slept with a peace she had never known before, and she owed it all to Bubbles. When she awoke the next morning, she realized that Bubbles was just a dream. In fact, none of the good things, as she remembered them, had ever really happened. However, Mary Ann did remember to smile that morning, hug her brother, dress with pride, and study for her test. Her life really did begin to magically get better and better.

We all have "Bubbles" inside us. We can choose to bring them out and be the best that we can be, or we can choose to lock them up inside, lost forever.

SAMUEL'S TREASURE

*S*wimming along the vast mountains and valleys of the ocean floor was a favorite pastime of Samuel's because in these deep crevasses lay some of the ocean's finest bounty. The ocean was full of treasure from sunken ships and lost civilizations and this hidden wealth belonged to the lucky explorer who found it first. Even though he was a starfish, he planned to explore all the oceans of the world, of course, Samuel had no idea that the oceans covered 2/3's of the earth's surface. He did know, however, that he would never tire of his daily search for sunken treasure.

His treasure chest was full of gifts from above, including coins, cans, necklaces, rings, bottles, and even a silver spoon. Samuel had no idea what a spoon was; however, its brilliant silver color and odd shape fascinated him. But none of his treasures was more precious than his Cool Ray sunglasses. When Samuel put on his Cool Rays his whole world changed color and for a Starfish to be able to change the color of his world was powerful stuff. Samuel and his friends would play for hours with all his treasures, except for Samuel's Cool Rays. No one wore the Cool Rays but Samuel.

Even underwater sea creatures have their favorite beaches where they go to play and relax. On just such an outing, Donnybrook, the giant Barracuda, paid Samuel a visit. While Samuel was relaxing in the sunlight, Donnybrook circled Samuel several times. Samuel knew that the Barracuda was up to no good, he just did not realize that he was to be the victim until Donnybrook dove down as fast as a bird snatches a bug and plucked Samuel's Cool Rays right off his face.

Samuel was mad, real mad and wanted to go after his sunglasses but knew better than to chase a Barracuda. The fact that Donnybrook was six feet long and had razor sharp teeth was reason enough for Samuel not to pursue him and demand his Cool Rays. Realizing there was nothing he could do, Samuel went home feeling sad and angry.

For days Samuel stayed close to home feeling sorry for himself. Even though he had a treasure chest full of fun things, all he could think about were his Cool Rays and that big bully Barracuda. Samuel's friends tried to get him to go hunt new treasure, but Samuel chose to stay home and brood. Soon his friends gave up and did not ask Samuel to play anymore.

TO HAVE A FRIEND, YOU MUST LEARN TO BUILD BRIDGES INSTEAD OF WALL...

Then one day Samuel's mother asked him, "Why don't you and your friends go on treasure hunts anymore?" Tears filled his eyes as he told his mom about Donnybrook stealing his sunglasses. With the love and patience only a mother has, Mrs. Starfish listened and waited for just the right time to comfort him.

"Let me see if I understand what you are telling me, Samuel," his mother said. "You have stopped playing with your friends, you no longer go treasure hunting, and you have abandoned the rest of your treasure, which took you years to gather—all the things you use to love—just because of one pair of sunglasses and one Barracuda."

Well Samuel hadn't looked at it quite like that. Samuel's mother went on, "No matter who you are or what you are, bad things happen to all of us. But there is something you can do about it. You can choose to forgive and forget, or you can choose to punish yourself for the wrongful actions of others."

"Punish myself?" Samuel questioned.

"That's right," she answered. "You have been punishing yourself by not playing with your other treasures and friends that you hold so dear."

Samuel knew his mother was right. He had been sad long enough, and it was time to enjoy the good things the sea had to offer.

It was already getting late and the afternoon sun was casting long shadows deep into the ocean, but Samuel headed out in search of treasure anyway. As he was swimming along a coral reef he spotted an old steamer trunk, still padlocked but showing signs of wear as only saltwater can do over a long period of time.

With little effort the nails came out of the soft wood and the padlock fell to the ocean floor. Samuel carefully opened the lid and squealed with delight. Inside the trunk was a large, sealed plastic bag which contained an assortment of sailor hats, more than enough to share with all his friends.

The next morning Samuel could hardly wait to see his friends and show them his newfound treasure. They were all so excited when Samuel opened his chest and pulled out the bag of hats. They immediately plunged into a game of pirates and sailors. Samuel laughed and told his friends, "That mean old Barracuda will never spoil my day again."

Even to this day, Samuel enjoys searching for lost treasure. Only now he realizes that life is too short to be unhappy about every little thing that goes wrong. The sea is full of treasures and friends.

Oh, by the way, that mean Barracuda soon tired of Samuel's Cool Rays and dropped them to the bottom of the ocean. If they should wash up on shore someday and you happen to find them, just throw them back into the water as far as you can. I'm sure one day Samuel will find them again.

IT'S WARMER BY THE FIRE

*T*he sky was clear, the air was cool, and the maple trees were covered in flaming red jackets. Yes, it was fall. Excitement filled the air as the geese headed south for the winter, and the chipmunks busily dashed from tree to tree storing up nuts for their long winter's nap. William was excited, too. He knew it wouldn't be long before his family took their annual ski trip. This was William's favorite time of the year. Thanksgiving break meant no school and no bedtime curfew; but best of all, it meant lots and lots of snow skiing. How exciting!

One night while William and his family were planning their ski trip, his dad got a phone call. "It sounds serious," William thought.

It was serious. William's grandfather had fallen, and he was no longer able to take care of himself. Papaw was moving into their house for a few months. William was excited. He loved his Papaw because his grandfather always took time to play and talk with him.

The house seemed a little strange at first with Papaw there all the time, but before long Papaw became a very important part of their lives. Every day he would sit by the window and watch William get on and off the school bus. William liked the thought that someone cared enough to wish him well every morning and be anxious for his return every afternoon. Papaw's jokes and stories were a welcomed relief after a long day at school.

William loved to take walks with Papaw and listen to stories about his father when he was a boy. Today's story was William's favorite tale about his dad and the frozen monkey bars. William sat down next to his grandfather as he began.

"Your father was around six years old with a bad case of cabin fever. It was very cold that day, well below freezing outside, and a winter storm had just dropped six inches of snow on the ground. As soon as the weather cleared up, he raced over to the park and started playing on the monkey bars. The hard cold metal was too inviting and your father decided to touch the metal bar with his tongue, just to see how cold it was. Much to his surprise, his wet tongue froze securely to the bar and he couldn't move or yell for help. His only alternative was to rip his tongue off the bar, leaving part of his tongue there. It was painful but a lesson well learned and never repeated."

After walking back to the house and eating dinner, the big news hit: no ski trip this year. William's dad gathered the family together, except for Papaw, and as lov-

THE WARMTH OF A FIRE NEEDS CONSTANT ATTENTION WHILE THE WARMTH OF A GRANDPARENT GLOWS ON ITS OWN.

ingly as he could, he explained that they must stay home this year to take care of Papaw. William was hurt and disappointed. "It's not fair!" he shouted as he ran from the room.

Quickly William's attitude toward papaw changed. He now resented Papaw's spying on him as he left for school and dreaded the afternoon stories. William was hurting inside. He could only see the world through his disappointment.

William and his father were raking leaves one afternoon when his father asked him to sit down for a moment. "I know you are hurting, Son," he said. "But Papaw is hurting, too. Gone is your grandfather's freedom and his independence. Can you imagine what life is like knowing you will never be able to take care of yourself again?"

William was so wrapped up in his own disappointment that he had never thought about how his grandfather was feeling. William desperately wanted to make up for all the terrible things he had said and thought. He loved his Papaw more than ever, because he now understood what his grandfather was going through. This Thanksgiving was going to be the best ever.

William jumped up, hugged his dad and ran to Papaw. "Come sit with me by the fire, Papaw. It is much warmer over here," William pleaded.

"No thanks," Papaw replied. "I just want to sit by the window and feel the sunshine. Besides, I have my quilt to keep me warm."

"That old quilt's not warm. Come sit by the fire with me," William begged.

Papaw motioned for William to come sit with him. As William settled down in Papaw's lap, the old gentleman pointed to the quilt and said, "This old quilt—let me tell you about this old quilt. It took your grandmother over a year to cut, piece, and stitch this quilt. You see this yellow square? That came from your baby blanket. Oh, the memories of you coming home from the hospital warms me to this day. This blue square was cut from your first pair of overalls. Do you remember wearing these when we would go fishing together? And this green patch came from your mother's first Sunday dress. How proud your mother was; you see, it was her first store-bought dress. Your grandmother never had such a dress. Warmer by the fire—I think not."

With tears in his eyes, Papaw continued on. "Every day for over a year your grandmother sat by the window and with God's light she lovingly made this old quilt. This quilt is a part of you, a part of me, and a part of your grandmother."

William now understood. Papaw had the warmth of Grandma in his heart, and the love and memories of her old quilt to keep him warm. Somehow that ski trip did not seem as important now, not nearly as important as knowing that Papaw would be by the window to welcome him home from school every day.

*N*ow that you have had an opportunity to experience all the stories, can you think of a better way to say, "I Love You?" *Worthy is the Child* is the perfect gift for holidays, birthdays, baby showers and especially when you just want to say "I Love You." Children quickly abandon new toys and continually outgrow even the best clothes, but as you can see, *Worthy is the Child* will keep on giving for the lifetime of both the parent and the child.

For a gift that keeps on giving, please consider the following offer:

- Additional copies of *Worthy is the Child* are $19.95 plus $4.00 S/H
- (1) Copy $23.95 Total
- (2) Copies $47.90 Total
- If you order 3 or more copies at $19.95 each (3 copies only $59.85 Total) we will pay all shipping and handling charges — a savings of at least $12.00 and the author will sign and date all copies and personalize the book with your loved ones names, should you include their names with your order.

Please make your Check or Money Order payable to NITE LITE STORIES, INC. If you would like to charge your order, please indicate, VISA or MASTERCARD and include your full account number and expiration date.

When you order please include the following:
- Your Complete Mailing Address
- Check/Money Order or VISA/MASTERCARD information
- How Many Books You Want
- Mail to:

Nite Lite Stories, Inc. Dept. 100
P. O. Box 12283
Jackson, MS 39236-2283

Please allow 4 to 6 Weeks for Delivery
Mississippi Residents Please include 7% Sales Tax

LIFE IS A GIFT. HOW YOU USE IT IS A BLESSING